OUT OF LOVE

"I called tonight—because I think we ought to make some sort of decision. Jill, I think we ought to break up," said Craig. "I can't believe I'm saying that. But do you see where I'm coming from?"

"Yes." A tear welled up in one of Jill's eyes and began to roll down her cheek.

"Do you—do you sort of agree with me?" Craig asked.

No, I don't, she thought frantically. *Now that it's finally happening, I don't want it. I don't!*

Jill felt as though her stomach were tumbling over and over. Her hands were trembling, and she was frightened.

I'm all alone now, she thought. *I loved him so much, and I lost him just because I chose Rosemont instead of State U.*

Bantam Books by Janet Quin-Harkin
Ask your bookseller for the books you have missed

Janet Quin-Harkin's

On Our Own

OUT OF
LOVE

Written by Eileen Hehl

BANTAM BOOKS
TORONTO · NEW YORK · LONDON · SYDNEY · AUCKLAND

RL 6, IL age 11 and up

OUT OF LOVE
A Bantam Book / August 1986

Sweet Dreams and its associated logo are registered trademarks of Bantam Books, Inc. Registered in U.S. Patent and Trademark Office and elsewhere.

Cover photo by Pat Hill

ISBN 0-553-25937-7

Published simultaneously in the United States and Canada

Bantam Books are published by Bantam Books, Inc. Its trademark, consisting of the words "Bantam Books" and the portrayal of a rooster, is Registered in U.S. Patent and Trademark Office and in other countries. Marca Registrada. Bantam Books, Inc., 666 Fifth Avenue, New York, New York 10103.

PRINTED IN THE UNITED STATES OF AMERICA

O   0 9 8 7 6 5 4 3

OUT OF
LOVE

ONE

Jill took a deep breath and forced herself to knock—three timid knocks—on the open door to the seniors' lounge in Phillips Hall. The room was filled with boys that evening, and many curious eyes turned toward her.

"Excuse me. My name is Jill Gardner, and I—"

"We know who you are," said one of the boys, giving her a bright, welcoming smile. "At least, I do." He was tall and sandy haired, with a few freckles on his nose. Somehow he didn't look old enough to be a college senior, but Jill didn't take time to ponder that. She was just surprised that he'd said he knew her.

Most of the boys were sprawled out on couches or the floor, watching a rerun of "M*A*S*H" on television. But the boy with the light sandy hair came over to the doorway to greet her.

"Sure, you're the Jill Gardner who writes that column in the Rosemont *Voice*," the boy said. He seemed to be proud of his knowledge. "You wrote

1

the infamous article about the terrible cafeteria food."

"Please, don't remind me," Jill groaned, remembering all the trouble and notoriety she'd received because of that one column.

"Don't be silly," said a voice from an unseen occupant in an overstuffed chair. "That was great satire."

"Well, thanks." Jill looked down as she blushed. As she regained her composure, she looked up and said, "Actually, I'm here because I'm writing a column this week about hometown romances, and I wonder if I might be able to interview a few of you. I need the upperclassmen to say a few things, to give me the 'voice of experience,' so to speak."

There. Jill had delivered her carefully rehearsed little speech after all. She still found it difficult going up to strangers, especially upperclassmen, to begin a conversation.

Now if her best friend Toni, from back home, had been there, it would have been a whole different scene.

"Hi, I'm Toni Redmond," Toni would have announced brightly. Then she would have plopped herself down in the midst of all the boys, smiling broadly and making herself right at home. "So, what is Hot Lips Houlihan up to this time?" she'd probably have quipped. And right away they would have welcomed her as a member of the group.

Jill sighed. Well, she was not Toni, and never would be. But she did need a story for that week's *Voice* column, and so she had forced herself to suppress her shyness and march bravely into the upperclass lounge.

"Sure, we'll let you interview us," a guy in sweatpants and a white T-shirt said. Jill couldn't help noticing they were all sort of cute. "But what did you say you're writing about? *Romances?*"

Jill blushed. "I know that sounds silly, but I couldn't figure out how else to put it. I mean, like, the girl you left behind, you know—the girl you dated back in high school and promised to stay true to—"

"Fascinating!" One of the seniors stood up and turned off the TV set. Now all eyes were glued on Jill. "Hey, grab a seat, Jill. This sounds like it could turn into a long evening."

It wasn't a long evening, but it was an eye-opener for Jill. One by one, almost every boy in the room answered her questions.

"The girl I left behind is *history*," said one boy, winking and looking not at all broken up about it. "That was three years ago, man! Did you think I was going to come to Rosemont to live like a monk?"

Another boy in aviator glasses said matter-of-factly, "My old high-school girlfriend dumped *me*. She was going to State U. and said there were just too many guys there. She couldn't stay faithful to me. *C'est la vie.*"

Jill was scribbling notes as fast as she could. But suddenly her mind started to wander. *State U. That's where Craig is. I wonder if the students at State feel the same way as these guys?*

"Life is too short," one of the seniors declared. "You have to make hay while the sun shines, as my granny says."

Jill jotted this down, too, corny as it sounded. Clichés were one thing she didn't need in her column. She was always aiming for a fresh and innovative approach.

Someone asked, "What do *you* say, Jake?" The boys all turned to look at a guy in khakis and a striped sweater sprawled sideways in the over-stuffed chair. Jill looked over at him. He was lean and dark haired, with sharp intelligent eyes, and his whole long body looked completely relaxed as he listened to the banter of the interview.

"That's Jake Randall," the boy in the aviators informed Jill. "*The* Jake Randall. You know, who writes all the great features every week in the *Voice*?"

Jill did, indeed, know the name Jake Randall. He was a legend on the Rosemont campus, and he hadn't even graduated yet. He was a good, prolific writer, and every issue of the *Voice* featured at least two or three of his polished pieces.

Suddenly she felt awkward and tongue-tied. *Oh, great! Jake Randall, of all people!* she thought. *Why did I have to pick THIS dorm?*

But Jake Randall turned out to be pleasant, even though he seemed to be keeping his distance. He smiled at Jill.

Look at him. He's trying to put the dumb little freshman at ease, Jill thought, clutching her pen and notebook more tightly.

"Just exactly what is it that you want to know?" Jake asked, coming right to the point.

"Oh. Well, most of these boys say that no romances seem to survive, after people are separated and go off to different colleges. The girls I've interviewed have mostly said the same thing. Do you—do you go along with that?"

She was thankful that her voice had come out clear and steady.

Jake Randall removed his legs from the arm of the chair and sat up straight. Everyone else in the room grew silent, like all the extras in the TV ad, waiting for E. F. Hutton to speak.

"I don't agree with that, Jill. I've been going with the same girl, Virginia, ever since high school. And she's away at Stanford, so we only see each other on holidays. But we're still faithful to each other, because we want to be. Totally."

"That's great," Jill blurted out impulsively, then realized how unprofessional she sounded. Did television interviewers, like Barbara Walters, gush every time someone made a statement? Of course not! But secretly, Jill did think it was touching. She liked knowing that somewhere in this maze of college students, there were two people who could have made a real commitment to each other.

"Thank you." Now Jill was trying to sound as professional as Barbara Walters as she looked around the room. "Anybody else want to comment?"

They all did.

"Yeah, don't swallow everything Jake says. He's feeding you a line!"

"He may have a girlfriend named Virginia, but he's never been faithful to her," a red-haired senior said, laughing. "Jake can make up some amazing stories, as you ought to know if you read his articles!"

They were all laughing, and Jill turned in confusion to Jake. He had sounded so sincere!

"I guess I have to plead guilty," he said in a strong, deep voice that was tinged with amusement. "I guess I am an incurable storyteller. And not just on paper."

"He's a playboy, too," the red-haired boy added. "The way he prowls around on this campus would make your head spin."

"I guess the joke is on me, then," Jill said, smiling. But she couldn't help feeling disappointed at not having found anyone at Rosemont who was faithful to an old high-school sweetheart.

"Yeah, Jake is full of it," the redhead summed up. "Nobody wants to hang on to last year's girl, no matter how great she might be."

She scribbled that down quickly: "Last year's girl." It might make a great title for her column.

"Being away at college is for meeting new people, man."

"When you're in college, the name of the game is dating plenty of girls."

And so on. Jill wrote it all down, then thanked the entire group once again. She had plenty of quotes to complete her column.

She was also bothered by a nagging, uneasy feeling. Maybe all these guys were right. Maybe this was the time for her to feel free to date other boys. And maybe—just maybe—it was time for Craig and her to break up.

"Bye, now," said the guy in sweatpants, waving at her from the floor. "Hey, come back and see us again sometime. You're not bad looking—for a freshman."

They were teasing her, and Jill laughed and went along with the gag. She also knew that she should get out of there right away. As she stuffed her pen and note pad back in her book bag, she thought to herself, *Toni wouldn't be leaving like this. She would have hung around and managed to wangle a date with practically every boy in the room—except for the formidable Jake Randall.*

The sandy-haired boy who had spoken to her first followed her out of the dorm. "I don't really belong here," he confided to Jill cheerfully, falling into step beside her. "I'm only a freshman, like you. I was just visiting a friend of my brother's."

"Oh," Jill said, smiling at him. She had thought he looked younger than the others. No wonder he hadn't offered any comments about hometown romances.

"My name is Terrence Lind," he said. "We're in the same psychology class, though you haven't noticed probably."

"I guess I haven't," Jill admitted. "I'm sorry. But it's only because psych is such a hard class for me." Jill shook her head. "Everything seems so intense here at Rosemont, doesn't it? And sort of—scary?"

"Yeah, but I figure that's the only way to learn. I like it here, so far."

"I do, too," Jill said in return. She felt comfortable with this boy. He seemed so sincere and honest, and he sounded like a serious student, not one of those party freaks like so many of the rich kids at Rosemont.

As they continued walking along together, Jill took a close look at Terrence Lind. A friendly, all-American-looking boy, he was dressed casually in a T-shirt and jeans, and his big feet were encased in well-worn sneakers.

"So, did you get enough stuff for your column?" Terrence asked.

"Oh, yes. Those quotes from the older guys were good. I think I even have a title for my column, from what they said—'Last Year's Girl.' Like it?"

Terrence smiled appreciatively. "I like it a lot. You know, I've been reading your columns ever since you started. In fact, I'd kind of like to do the same thing, one of these days."

"You mean you want to write for the *Voice*? You ought to go talk to Russel. He's the editor who gave me a chance in September." Jill grinned. "It was funny how it happened. Russel was desperately trying to fill four inches of column space, and I happened to stumble into his office at the right time."

"No kidding?"

"Yes, really. He told me to write something, anything funny, and I did—on the spot. That's how I became a columnist." She looked up at Terrence. "And the rest, as they say, is history." She was pleased when he laughed at her little joke.

"I'll go and talk to Russel, then. Thanks, Jill." Terrence put his hands into the front pockets of his jeans. "I want to be a writer more than anything in the world."

"So do I, I think," Jill said. "I'm enjoying doing my column, but there are times when I get discouraged, knowing my pieces will never measure up to any of the stuff that Jake Randall writes."

"I know. I guess he's sort of my idol. He sure whips up a story like no one else can."

Terrence showed no signs of leaving Jill's side as she walked back to McGregor, her dorm, slowly. She wondered if he intended to follow her all the way to McGregor. She was surprised to realize that she didn't mind a bit.

"I like this time of evening at Rosemont," Jill said softly. Everything at the college was bathed in dusky darkness as early night settled over the campus, lengthening the shadows.

"Me, too," Terrence agreed.

Jill loved the old ivy-covered buildings and the long stretches of manicured lawn that always smelled freshly mowed. She loved the few modern buildings, too, that stood out here and there in dramatic relief against the original low brick structures.

"It's a fantastic school," Terrence said quietly.

Jill turned to look at her new friend. "You know, it really is. I had a lot of doubts about coming here. I—I was supposed to go to State U. with my best friend, Toni, and my boyfriend, Craig."

"And? What changed your mind?" Terrence seemed genuinely interested.

Jill reflected. "First of all, Toni's father got sick, and she decided she'd be better off going to a school right in Seattle, a local community college. I'm from Seattle, by the way. And then Craig—"

She hesitated. "Craig really wanted me to be at State with him—he's a sophomore there this year—but I sort of realized that I needed a little space. Just some distance, since we'd been going out for over a year."

"I suppose he's carved out his own life, there at State," Terrence guessed.

"Yes, exactly." Jill was amazed that this boy seemed to read her mind. "I met a bunch of his friends one night at a party, and I knew, somehow, that if I went to State, I'd end up being just an appendage to Craig."

"And you wanted to be your own person," Terrence finished for her. "I know what you mean.

10

And that's probably the reason why you're doing this column about 'Last Year's Girl.'"

"You know, you're right about that, too," Jill said. "I've been thinking about breaking up with Craig. Oh, I know that sounds cruel, but it's not, really. We both agreed that we should date other people, and—"

She waited. She almost expected Terrence to finish that sentence for her, too. But he was silent, looking at her intensely.

"Oh, well, enough about me," Jill said. They were almost at her dorm now, and she was interested in learning something about Terrence. "What about you? Are you—"

She never got to finish. Her roommate, Cassandra, popped her head out of the window of their first-floor room.

"Jill, hurry up. Telephone for you!"

"I'll be there in just a minute, Cass—"

"No, you've got to hurry. It's your friend Toni, from back home, and she says she's in a big hurry. Emergency!"

"Okay." Jill looked regretfully at Terrence. "Everything with Toni is always in a hurry and a big emergency. But I'd better run and see what it's all about."

"Sure. We'll talk again some other time," Terrence said amiably. "So long, Jill."

She watched him amble away with his long-legged stride. *What a nice, interesting boy,* she thought. There was something vaguely familiar

11

about Terrence, yet she was fairly sure she'd never met him before. It must be because he was in her psychology class.

And then she ran up the McGregor porch stairs, two at a time, to see what Toni's latest crisis was.

TWO

"Jill?" Toni's voice came over the phone in its usual impatient way. "Is that you, Jill?"

Jill was totally breathless. She'd nearly killed herself racing to the phone, slamming against two corners and one banister in her haste to find out about Toni's emergency.

Puffing, Jill tried to answer. "Yes—it's me. Is that you, Toni?"

"Of course it is, silly," came back the impatient reply. "Who did you think it was?"

"Toni—" Jill took a deep breath. She looked down at her body and wondered just how many bruises she had acquired on this frantic dash. "What's wrong? What's the emergency?"

Toni laughed. "Oh, there really isn't one. But it was the only way I could get that roommate of yours to go looking for you. She certainly sounds stubborn."

"Toni Redmond! Do you mean to tell me that you made me rush all that way— Do you mean to tell me that you let me get black-and-blue from head to toe—and there is no emergency at all?"

"Well, in a way there is," Toni said blithely. "After all, my finances are always in a state of emergency. So if you didn't hurry up, I'd be stuck with a humongous telephone bill, and I couldn't afford that. You know I couldn't."

Jill couldn't help laughing. "Oh, Toni, you're crazy. And you know what? I miss you so much! How are things in Seattle?"

"Fine, just fine," Toni said expansively. "You know me—I'm always on top of things. Well, almost always. Maybe I'm not getting all A's in school, but that's nothing new, is it?"

"And how about your job at the theater?"

"Couldn't be better. They'd just fall apart without me at that place. Why, yesterday I did all the filing and almost got as far as the letter *G*—"

"Sounds exciting, Toni," Jill remarked dryly. "How about you and Brandt?"

"Ah, now you're talking, Jill. Now there's an area where all is truly mellow. I mean, there is *nothing* like an older man—but how about you? Have you met any cute guys yet?"

Jill hesitated. "No, not really."

"What does that mean? You have been going out, haven't you?"

"Well—once in a while. Not very often, actually. I guess I've still been feeling involved with Craig, so I haven't gotten around much—"

"*Involved with Craig?!*" Toni's voice came across the phone as a loud shriek. "I thought you guys decided to cool it! You *know* he's messing around

14

with other girls at State, Jill. What's the matter with you?"

"Nothing. I mean, I would go out—if someone comes along, I would. Oh, I don't know, it bothers me because Craig and I didn't formally break up, or anything."

There was an ominous silence from Toni's end. "Jill, I'm going to tell you something for your own good. It's time, right now, for you to get in touch with Craig and bite the bullet. Break it off, once and for all. Otherwise you'll never give any other guys a chance."

Jill sighed. "I know you're right, Toni. I've been thinking the same thing myself. Of course I hate to hurt Craig—"

"He'll survive," Toni said curtly. "You've got to do it, Jill. There's a whole world of gorgeous men out there for you to meet—and I do purposely use the word *men,* not *boys*—"

Jill suddenly remembered Terrence. "Hey, I did meet a cute boy today, and he walked me home. He's a freshman, though."

"Ditch him. Bag him. Forget him." As always, when Toni was giving advice, she was starting to get too pushy. "You want to go for someone *older,* Jill. Older men have so much more experience, and panache—"

"*Panache,* Toni?"

"Sure. I read it in a magazine. It means style, or charm or something. Probably whatever goes along with maturity."

15

"Is that Brandt's big attraction? Being a Joe Panache?"

"No, of course not. Brandt is—Brandt. Exciting, debonair, lovable. Jill, promise me that you'll call Craig and settle this. Tonight?"

"I think I will. I think I'm ready now, Toni."

"Excellent! You'll never be sorry. Listen, I'm going to have to hang up now, or pretty soon the phone company will be repossessing my telephone."

"I'm glad you called. You could write once in a while, too, you know."

"Yuck. You're the writer, Jill, not me. Anyway, I'm so busy being Suzy Homemaker here in my cozy little apartment—whoops! I hear a terrible noise."

"What is it?"

"It might be those eggs I put on to boil for my dinner. That was an awful long time ago. I wonder if the water might have boiled down?"

"Oh, Toni. You should use a timer so you won't forget things like that."

"Too late now! I hear explosions going on all over my kitchen. Oh, gross. Bye, Jill."

Jill heard the click as Toni put the receiver down.

"That's so typical of Toni," Jill said with a sigh, returning to her room. She found Cassandra sitting in a yoga position on the scatter rug. "There wasn't any emergency at all. At least not until her whole kitchen started to explode, from overboiled eggs."

Cassie laughed heartily. "Toni sounds like a real character," she observed. "I hope I get to meet her someday." Jill watched as her roommate maneuvered her limbs so that she was finally, effortlessly, standing on her head.

Who's calling who a character? Jill thought with amusement. But she was fond of Cassandra and felt so lucky to have her as a roommate. Offbeat as Cassandra might be, with her long, dark straight hair and her far-out wardrobe, she was terrific fun and never dull.

When Jill thought of herself, she figured that she came across as the quiet, cautious, conservative type—but for some reason she always seemed to gravitate toward zany friends. First Toni, and now this upside-down person practicing the yoga that she had learned in India.

"I know you'll like Toni, when you two finally get to meet," Jill said confidently. "You're not at all alike. But somehow you both seem to be willing to put up with me, and that's what counts."

"Jill, I have a feeling you've got more important things to worry about than whether your two friends like each other. Right?" Cassandra said, her body wobbling as she struggled to stay on her head. "Something tells me you've got Craig on your mind."

It was hard to talk to someone whose chin was above her eyebrows. But Jill tried. "Yes, you're right about that. I've been debating about breaking up with him. I guess I'm just a coward!"

"I'd tell you to call him and talk to him right now, except that I'm not the interfering type."

"You're right, Cassandra. Maybe I could get Craig on the phone now. It's past dinner time, but not really party time yet, if that's what they're doing tonight at the Sigma house."

"Good luck, then, Jill." Cassandra toppled over just then, laughing at herself as she barely missed crashing into her bed. "Guess I've gotten a little out of practice with my advanced positions," she said.

Jill walked down the hall to the phone and dialed Craig's number. She had it memorized, even though she hadn't called him much this semester. Her heart began to hammer wildly inside her chest.

"Hello? This is Mark's Bar and Grill," said a voice at the other end of the line.

"Hi, Mark," Jill said evenly to Craig's wacky fraternity brother. "This is Jill Gardner. Is—is Craig around?"

"He sure is, honey child. Hold on."

Craig's voice came on next, sounding warm and welcoming. "Jill. What a nice surprise!"

He sounds so wonderful, Jill thought dismally. *And I've loved him for so long. How can I even think of doing this?*

"Hi, Craig. How are you?"

"I'm fine, Jill, but—I miss you. I never realize how much until I hear your voice on the phone, and then—well, never mind that. How are *you*?"

"Okay. Listen, I—"

"Yes?"

18

"I—I wondered how your studies are coming along."

"Oh, fine, hon. I'm working hard, really hard. How about you?"

I'm thinking about you—a lot, Jill thought. *Too much*.

"Everything okay with you, Jill?" Craig sounded worried.

"Oh—yes, sure." Jill knew suddenly that she couldn't do it. Not like this. Not when Craig was sounding so loving and concerned about her. It was impossible.

"You haven't written lately," Craig said quietly. "I remember when you used to write to me almost every day."

"That was when I was still in high school," Jill said. "I'm a lot busier, now—now that I'm in college."

"I know." Craig sighed. "It really is a whole different world, isn't it? You'll never guess what I'm doing this season."

"What?"

"Something really crazy. Learning fencing at a special night class. You know, sword fighting, but with blunt tips so no one gets hurt."

"That sounds great. It's a sport I've always admired." Jill really meant it. She thought it was a pretty weird sport, but it was elegant. She could just imagine Craig, swashbuckling in a tight white costume and wire face mask, holding one of those

19

foils. "I never seem to get involved in anything physically exciting," she said as an afterthought.

"Well, maybe you ought to, sometime," Craig told her enthusiastically. "You're probably more athletic than you think. I remember how good you always were at swimming. Oh, and I hope you'll send me some more of your columns, Jill. I really love reading them."

Why does he have to be so nice? Jill thought. *I've got to break up with him, and yet he's making it impossible.*

They talked for a few minutes more, and then Craig had to run. He'd be late for his fencing class, he said. They said quick goodbyes.

Cassandra, back in their room, was looking flushed and triumphant as she always did after her yoga workout. "So—you don't look upset or anything," she said to Jill. "I guess he took it okay?"

"Mmmmm." Jill pretended to be busy looking for an English book.

"Mmmmm? Do you know what 'mmmmm' sounds like?" Cassandra stood with her hands on her hips, staring at Jill curiously. "It sounds to me as if you failed to carry out your mission."

"Mmm-hmmmm," said Jill with emphasis. Then she faced Cassandra and broke into a grin, in spite of herself. "You are looking at the world's biggest idiot. I'm chicken, I'm a wimp, and I'm a total cop-out. But I can't help it."

Cassandra looked quietly sympathetic, and Jill was grateful, for once, that Toni wasn't there. Toni would have bawled her out. In fact, Toni probably would have charged over to the phone and called Craig herself, to settle the matter.

It's nice to have a different kind of friend, at times, Jill mused. *Especially at a moment like this, when I feel so confused.*

"I guess I'll start writing my *Voice* column," Jill said. "It'll keep me busy for a while."

"Sure," Cassandra said. "And I guess I'll take my usual walk around campus and see if the muse visits me. I haven't written a good poem in a long time. See you later, roomie."

THREE

"Hey, where've you been?" called out a male voice. Jill was just leaving the cafeteria after breakfast the next day, and she was still thinking about Craig and the phone call.

"We're going to be late," the voice said.

It was Terrence Lind, and he was looking at Jill as though she had flipped out or something.

"Late for what?" Jill was mystified.

"Are you serious? Have you forgotten that you signed up for that psychology experiment this morning?"

Jill's mouth formed a perfect O. "I did forget. I've had so much on my mind this week—" Jill stopped suddenly and stared up at Terrence, noticing for the first time that he had sparkling green eyes. "Wait a minute. How'd you know I signed up?"

Terrence grinned, and he looked really cute standing next to the ivy-covered dining hall, with splotches of sunlight playing in his sandy-colored hair.

"Because I signed up, too, of course. Well, come on. If we miss this one, we may not get another chance. And we have to be in at least two psych experiments to pass the course."

"I know." Jill hurried to keep up with Terrence's long-legged stride. She was annoyed with herself for forgetting something as important as this. It really wasn't like her.

"Thanks for reminding me, Terrence," she panted as they charged along the path toward the psychology building.

"Think nothing of it."

They entered the psychology building, and, as always, Jill had to stop to get her bearings. The modern building was designed in somewhat of a maze shape.

"You have to be a trained rat to find your way around this place," Jill grumbled as they traipsed down the hall, looking for their room.

"Only we're not looking for cheese—we're looking for inkblots." Terrence was grinning wildly.

"Hey, here it is," Jill called out, reading a sign on the door of room 106. "Inkblots." They both stopped short and looked at each other. Jill whispered, "Are we sure we want to go through with this?"

"They might find out that we're severely paranoid and psychotic, huh?" Terrence was smiling cheerfully.

"Psychotic? Speak for yourself." Jill gave Terrence a push through the doorway. "I probably fit into the neurotic category, myself."

The room was filled with Psych 101 students. A movie screen had been set up at the front of the classroom, and some chairs were arranged in a semicircle around the screen.

"Well, it doesn't look too ominous," Jill said. "I guess they aren't going to wire our brains or try to wipe out our memories."

She must have spoken more loudly than she intended because a number of the students laughed. Just as Jill and Terrence did, they all looked slightly nervous—not knowing what to expect.

"They'd have to shave our heads if they planned to wire our brains," suggested one of the boys sitting in the semicircle.

"So I guess we're safe from that—*this* time," Terrence said. He gestured to Jill to sit down, then he sat down next to her.

A young man who looked vaguely familiar to Jill entered the room. He was of medium height, with a dark beard and thick, dark hair. His eyes looked almost black under thick eyelashes.

If Toni were here she'd say, "Wow, who's that handsome creature? Get his name, rank, and serial number—quick!" Jill thought. She found herself wanting to know his name, herself; the guy was really interesting looking. Jill's mouth felt dry, just looking at him.

She left out the "wow" and asked Terrence, "Who's he?"

"He's the teacher's assistant, or T.A. Haven't you seen him before?"

"Yes, somewhere."

"He's just a student, like the rest of us, but he earns extra credit by doing a lot of the tedious work for

24

a professor. Ryan doesn't always show up for every psych class, but he's always available to help us freshman students."

Jill stared at the fascinating man as he took command of the room. "But—how can he be an undergraduate like us? He looks so old."

"Ryan?" Terrence appeared to be thinking about her question. "He is older than all the other students. I don't know why. He probably started late. But he's only a junior, I think."

Only a junior—how interesting, Jill thought. She was intrigued. *Ryan—what?* she wondered. But she didn't have a chance to ask Terrence.

"All right, people," said Ryan, standing informally in front of the movie screen. He had the sort of voice that commanded attention right away. The whole room quieted down.

"Time to get started. I assume you all were on the sign-up list for inkblots?"

"We were," called out Bob Bates, one of the comedians of the class. "But we're not sure we qualify. Don't you have to be a real nut case before you do inkblot tests?"

Ryan stared meaningfully at Bob. "You don't have to worry about qualifying, in that case," he said simply. The entire group roared with laughter, and some of the tension evaporated.

Ryan makes a really good teacher, Jill thought with admiration. She wondered why her heart was doing funny little flip-flops whenever she looked at him, though. She'd never had a crush on a teacher before.

The experiment was about to begin. "Now, what I'll do is show you two movies," Ryan explained.

"Are they rated G or X?" asked Bob, trying for another laugh. He got a few.

"I'll ignore that," Ryan said with a thin smile. "I'll show you the first film—it's only a few minutes long—and then we'll get into the inkblots."

The T.A. dimmed all the lights, pulled down the window shades, and manned the projector from the back of the classroom.

"Oh, goody, it's a sinking-ship disaster movie," someone yelled out as gently lapping ocean waves filled the movie screen.

Ryan switched off the movie. He sounded as though he were running out of patience now.

"Anyone who feels the need to talk during the film will be expelled from the room," he stated firmly. "Is that clear?"

It was. The group settled down to watch the movie in silence.

Jill was having trouble concentrating on the movie, although it was full of pretty, peaceful scenes such as mountain ranges and sand dunes, a Midwest cornfield and a giant redwood forest.

Why can't I concentrate? she wondered. And then she realized that she was much more interested in the forceful young man who was running the projector than in the movie he was showing!

Well, at least I'm not thinking about Craig, she thought. *That's a nice change.*

She wasn't thinking about Craig later, either, when Ryan turned on the lights again and held up the various inkblots, which were on large cards.

"All right, I'll go around the semicircle for each card," Ryan said. "You—on my right. What do you see here?"

The freshman girl looked confused. "Ink," she said.

There were giggles all around her.

"Well, yes, of course you see ink," Ryan said amiably. "But the design is supposed to remind you of something. Does it look like anything recognizable to you?"

The girl concentrated. "Well, it looks like a ketchup stain I once had on my uniform at work. You see, I was a waitress for the summer, and they started using these squeeze bottles on the counters, and—"

"Very good. Thank you." Ryan seemed to be amused. "Next student, please."

Bob was next. He made a big show of concentrating fiercely. "That inkblot looks like—" He paused for effect. "It looks like an octopus, to me."

"Fine. Next person, please."

Jill was next. She could feel Ryan's intense eyes on her, and it was almost as though they were boring into her. She felt oddly nervous.

"The inkblot looks like a starfish, I think," she said.

And so on, across the room they went. After five inkblot cards, Ryan showed a different sort of movie, one that was full of unpleasant scenes such as storms and volcanoes, flooded valleys, and even violent war scenes.

Then Ryan held up the inkblot cards, the same ones, Jill noticed, as the time before. This time people answered differently.

"That's a lethal weapon," one student said of the starfish-ketchup-stain-octopus inkblot. Another called it a stab wound. Another saw it as a hole blasted in the earth by dynamite.

Jill realized suddenly what the experiment had been about—how a different mood can make a person see things differently.

When the session was over, Terrence made the same observation to her. "Interesting, isn't it? People perceive things totally differently after a certain type of conditioning," he said.

"Yes." Jill was reluctant to leave the room. She wanted to think of something to say to the T.A., but he was busy with several other students. She could see that he wouldn't be free for quite a while.

Sighing, she left the psychology building with Terrence.

"That was fun," Terrence said, strolling along beside Jill. "So how are you coming along with your column for this week?"

I wonder why he's always so interested in what I'm doing, Jill thought.

"Oh, pretty well. I have that hometown romance story all finished and handed in." She gave a short laugh. "I wish I could solve my personal problems as

28

easily as I bat out that column," she said before she could stop herself.

But Terrence was perceptive enough not to ask her any more, and she was glad. "Here's where I turn off for my next class," he said. "If you need help—I mean, if you need to talk about any personal problems or anything, give me a call. I live in Hollister Hall."

"Thanks, Terrence. But I think I'll have to come up with my own solutions. After all, that's one of the reasons I'm here at Rosemont, far away from Craig and Toni—and my parents. I need to learn to work out things for myself."

Terrence looked down at her without saying anything. Jill suddenly had the feeling that he was attracted to her—at least, she thought so.

Oh, why was everything so mixed up? Here she was, eager to break up with Craig, and yet she couldn't do it. Here was Terrence wanting to be better friends with her, and yet she couldn't help thinking he was too young for her. And there was that hunk, Ryan. She'd love to get to know him better, even though he must be at least twenty-two years old.

At the moment, it was too much to sort out. Jill squared her shoulders and strode purposefully along the campus path. She didn't want to be late for Dr. Holloman's English class, her favorite subject in her whole schedule.

FOUR

"Phone call for you, Jill," called out Marcie, an older girl on her floor. Marcie greeted Jill as she stepped into the McGregor lounge after coming in from dinner. Jill had been planning to take a quick shower and then get over to her job at the copy shop.

"Sounds like an awful cute male-type voice," Marcie added with a wink. "Might even be long distance—and I know who that would be!" Most of the girls in McGregor knew that Jill had a hometown boyfriend who went to State U.

Jill went to one of the phones that hung on the wall of the outer lounge. She was surprised to find that it *was* Craig.

"Well, hi, Craig," she said. "This is unexpected. Two calls in two days. You're making my dormmates jealous."

"Hi, Jill." Craig sounded subdued, and right away a little warning bell began to go off in Jill's head.

"Is anything wrong?" she asked. "You sound so—strange. Is somebody sick, or anything?"

30

"No, it's nothing like that—" answered Craig in a too-quiet voice—"it's just, well, I've been doing a lot of thinking, since we talked last night."

"So have I," Jill said warily. "But what—?"

"It's this, Jill." Craig's voice became more forceful, suddenly, as though he had just summoned up a new reserve of courage to get him through the phone call. "I've been thinking, well, this isn't working out too well. You know what I mean?"

"I—I'm not sure."

"I mean—you and me, still being in love but being so far away. It just—well, it just isn't working, Jill."

"But—well—what can we do? I couldn't transfer to State now, even if I wanted to, which I don't. Craig, you know that—"

"I know you can't, Jill. That's just my point. We're not going to be together for the next four years, and—I don't know about you, but I've been having trouble with that."

Jill whispered, "I've been having trouble with it, too, Craig."

Craig sighed deeply. "Remember how we said we should both be free to date other people? Well, I never feel I *am* free, Jill. I keep thinking that you're my girl and I'm supposed to stay faithful."

"Same here," she echoed.

"So I called tonight—because I think we ought to make some sort of decision. Jill, I think we ought

31

to break up. I can't believe I'm saying that. But do you see where I'm coming from?"

"Yes." A tear welled up in one of Jill's eyes and began to roll down her cheek.

"Do you—do you sort of agree with me?" Craig asked.

No, I don't, she thought frantically. *Now that it's finally happening, I don't want it. I don't!*

But when she spoke she said just the opposite. "I think I do, Craig."

"And you won't hate me or anything?"

"How could I ever hate you?" She felt more tears coming and wished she had a tissue handy.

"We were really good for each other, Jill, but you see, we've got to have the experience of going out with other people."

"Absolutely," she said automatically.

"And then, when the four years are up, maybe—well, who knows? Maybe we'll have time then to get reacquainted."

"Sounds good." Her nose was beginning to run, too, but she struggled to make her voice sound chipper and bright. "Hey, I guess we have a tentative date, then—four years from now."

"Are you all right, Jill? You're crying, aren't you?"

"Of course I'm crying," she said carefully. "What do you expect, Craig? I've loved you for a long time."

"I know. Same here."

A long silence strung out between them. Finally Craig went on. "I'll probably always love you, Jill, but we won't ever be certain until—well, you know. Four years from now."

"Sure. Four years from now."

"Well, if you're sure you're okay. Are you?"

"I will be." She sniffed. "Craig?"

"What?"

"Take care of yourself."

"I will. You, too, you hear?"

Neither of them wanted to hang up. So Jill took the initiative. "Oh, I have to get over to my job. Bye, now, Craig." And she put down the receiver.

Jill felt as though her stomach were tumbling over and over, just like the clothes in a washing machine. Her hands were trembling, and she was frightened.

I'm all alone now, she thought. *I loved him so much, and I lost him just because I chose Rosemont instead of State U.*

She had made up her mind not to cry, but the tears were forming anyway. It was such a final break, she thought. Craig was doing it in the kindest way possible, and for the best of reasons—for them both—but it just sounded so final. That stuff about four years! Who did he think he was fooling?

"I'll see you in four years," she whispered out loud, tasting the bitterness of those words.

"Huh? Did you say something, Jill?" Marcie was standing at the archway near the bank of telephones, holding a quarter in her hand. No doubt she was waiting to call out for a Weird Willie's pizza.

"No, I guess I didn't say anything, Marcie," Jill said firmly. She lifted her chin. She really shouldn't cry, or give in to self-pity, at least not at the moment. She had to go to work at the copy shop. If she could get through the next few hours without breaking down, then she knew she would prove to herself that she was starting to be truly mature, as a college student was supposed to be.

But, oh, it hurt so much!

She went to her room feeling like a zombie. Cassandra was nowhere in sight. Methodically Jill took her shower, then headed over to the student press, where the copy shop was.

"Hi, Jill," called out Mr. Allen, the print-shop manager. "Boy, am I glad to see you! My best little worker. We've got so much to do this evening—hey, are you feeling all right? You look a bit pale."

"I'm fine," Jill said in her steadiest voice. "Just pile the work on." *Work may be the best remedy for heartbreak*, she told herself.

But for the first time in her life, Jill began to feel as though she were the accident-prone Toni instead of herself. Everything she did was a disaster. She dropped a huge stack of flyers that Mr. Allen had just printed, and some of them got soiled on the inky part of the floor.

She ran off copies for students and found herself pushing all the wrong buttons: Extra-dark copies when the copies were perfectly legible, and legal-size paper when letter sized was called for.

"Oh, gosh, I'm so sorry," she kept saying, both to customers and to Mr. Allen with each new mistake she made.

"This just isn't like you, Jill," Mr. Allen finally said. "I really do think you're sick—or coming down with something. You know, there's been a lot of flu going around this campus. Do you have a fever?"

"I don't have the flu, Mr. Allen," Jill said, and just then she backed into a desk and sent a stack of just printed copies of the *Voice* flying all over the room. She scrambled madly to pick them all up, feeling her face turn red.

This must be the way Toni feels all the time, Jill thought. Toni had always been accident prone. But bumbling around like this was certainly a new and terrible experience for Jill.

Finally Mr. Allen stopped Jill just as she was about to do a giant copying job for a professor.

"Jill, no—please. We can't afford to have a problem with the copy machine. If it jams, or if it stops altogether—"

"I'll be careful, Mr. Allen, really."

"No." Firmly he took the manuscript away from her. "Listen, I know you're always a good worker. But something has upset you tonight—don't deny it, I can tell. So I want you to take the rest of the evening off, Jill."

"But—you need me tonight—"

"I'll call Bob in—or Kevin. I'll find somebody who can take over for you." Mr. Allen's kind face was filled with concern. "Look, you go on over to the student union. Maybe have an ice-cream cone or something. Laugh a little, talk to someone. I'm sure you'll feel better."

Jill hung her head for a moment, and then she remembered her new motto, "No Self-Pity."

"Okay, Mr. Allen. I'll take your advice. Thank you, and—I'm really sorry about tonight."

Trudging across campus, ignoring the beauty of Rosemont at night, Jill was aware of a deep ache in her chest. She was trying to avoid thinking about Craig, but her body was betraying her by reminding her with this pain.

She began to wonder if she was responsible for the breakup. *I'm such a wishy-washy person*, she thought. *I've always known that I'm too cautious. Maybe that's why I lost the boy I loved most in the whole world.*

It made sense. There was Craig, learning to fence, of all things, and what was she doing with herself? Nothing more exciting than writing a weekly column, helping to edit the literary magazine, and working in a boring old copy shop. Correction: *destroying* the boring old copy shop.

No wonder I lost Craig! she thought. She had always tried not to be stodgy and cautious like her married sister, Stephanie, but maybe she'd only succeeded as well as she had because she had had crazy, adventurous Toni around to inspire her. Now that she was on her own, she was well on her way to becoming a total washout.

That was the frame of mind she was in as she entered the student union, the large campus gathering place for Rosemont kids on their free time. Everywhere she saw groups of boys and girls, studying, laughing, sipping sodas, or eating—tight little gatherings, groups of friends. Jill had never felt so alone in her entire life.

"Hey," someone called out to her. "Do you want to join the chess club? We're looking for more members."

Jill shuddered. Did she look like the type who'd be recruited for the chess club?

"No, thank you," she said politely and walked on.

"Hello," said another student. "We're having club recruiting for the second time here tonight. It'll give you a second chance to join up. Would you like to join?"

"What's your club?"

"The R.P.S."

Jill stopped for a moment by the table where the eager club members sat. "What does that stand for?"

"Rosemont Philatelic Society. We have a great time. It's a way to meet new people and pursue your hobby—"

"Philatelic? *Stamps?* Doesn't philatelic mean stamps?" Jill was horrified, but she tried to keep her voice from betraying it.

"Sure, stamp collecting. We have meetings every week, and—"

"I'm sorry," Jill said interrupting. "I'm not—I don't—" Oh, how could she put it in a civilized way? "I really am very busy, with my other activities." She hurried away from them as though afraid that they'd come charging after her with a butterfly net. But, no, that would be the entomology club, wouldn't it?

These club recruiters were not improving her mood at all. In fact, they were depressing her even more. She decided she'd better get clear of them before she was accosted by the coin collectors or the checkers club.

But another voice stopped her before she could run.

"Hey, you there with the gorgeous chestnut hair," a boy called out. "Yes, you. Can you swim?"

Here we go again, Jill thought. "Yes, I can swim, but—"

"How'd you like to play water polo?"

Jill stopped dead in her tracks. "Water polo—" She had heard of the game, but had never seen it played. It sounded exciting, and fast, and utterly collegiate. In fact, maybe as interesting as Craig's fencing!

"You have a water polo club?"

"Yep, and we need players," a blond girl said. "You don't need experience. All you need is a Speedo racing suit and the ability to keep from drowning."

"Suzie," the boy scolded. "She has to be a good swimmer. A really strong swimmer who can take all the rigorous training—"

"I am!" Jill burst out. "I have my senior lifesaving certificate, and I was on the swim team in junior high school for a while."

"Great," said the team captain, who introduced himself as Paul. "Because it really is a demanding sport, and you'll need to get into good shape."

"Where do I sign up?" she asked impulsively. And immediately she felt her spirits lift. *Uh, oh,* she thought. *Cautious Jill Gardner is going to do something adventurous for a change—play water polo!*

She grinned at Paul, a guy with a husky build, who told her that the co-ed club played informally against other colleges. It was not really a varsity sport, as such.

"Hey, welcome to the group," the blond girl said as Jill signed her name to a recruiting list. "You'll really like it, I think. Be at practice at eleven in the morning, whenever you don't have an eleven o'clock class. It's the main pool in the field house."

"Okay." Jill was smiling, pleased with herself for the first time all evening. "I'll be there!"

FIVE

I don't believe I just did that, Jill thought as she headed for the student union coffee shop. For a moment panic overtook her. Water polo—she had really signed up to play a wild game like water polo!

What had she done? Well, something good, maybe. She had just acted adventurous and unconventional—the way Toni might have. The difference, of course, was that whenever Toni lost something important to her—namely, a boyfriend—she staged a two- or three-hour drama of tears, hysterics, and wailing.

I'm glad I'm not wailing and crying, Jill thought proudly. She'd been quite calm through it all, in spite of the mishaps at the copy shop. She had stayed pretty levelheaded and free from tears, and the only crazy thing she'd done was to sign up for a club.

"I'll have a giant banana split, please," Jill suddenly found herself saying to the boy behind the ice-cream counter. "With lots of whipped cream and some nuts, and plenty of strawberries all around the bananas."

I must be crazy! she thought in horror. Jill never ate banana splits; she couldn't remember ever having had one in her whole life. A small sundae, maybe, now and then, but a whole giant banana split? All that disgusting sweet stuff and the thousands of calories that nobody needed?

But, unbelievably, she had ordered one, and the boy was in the act of putting it together right then. Jill knew her face was turning red. She just wasn't behaving like herself that night.

"Guess you must be hungry," the boy said as he began squashing the whipped cream onto the ice cream and fruit. "What did you do, skip dinner?"

"No, I had dinner. I think." Dinner seemed so long ago that Jill couldn't remember what she'd eaten. Her head was pounding, and she was totally confused. Her whole world had turned upside down in the short space between dinner and then.

She paid for the banana split and carried it to a table, being careful not to spill the towering concoction.

"This is gross," she whispered out loud to herself, and yet she began digging in with the long-handled spoon. The whipped cream seemed overly sweet, but the ice cream itself tasted soothing and cool. Jill attacked the banana split as if it were the last food she'd ever see.

Then suddenly the tears began.

She couldn't stop them. She was horrified to see big, fat teardrops splashing down into the whipped cream and nuts.

She couldn't eat, anyway. There was too big a lump in her throat. A terrible thought hit her: what if she never fell in love again? Or worse—what if no one ever loved her again? What if there was no one in the whole wide world who could capture her heart the way Craig had? What if she was alone, forever and ever, not just in college but all through her long miserable life?

"Excuse me," said a deep voice from behind her. "I hope you don't mind my intrusion, but I can see that something is wrong, and I believe I know you from somewhere."

Jill looked up, ready to say that she wasn't in the mood to talk to *anyone*, and couldn't he see that?!

But she never got the words out. The man standing there was Ryan, the bearded T.A. from her psychology class. And if she had thought he was good-looking before, he looked sensational to her then! He was wearing brown: brown cotton chinos and a lighter brown shirt, open at the throat. The outfit emphasized the rich chocolate of his eyes and almost made them sparkle.

"I'm probably not welcome," he said in that wonderful deep voice that she had admired when he stood in front of the psych class. "I'll leave you alone if you'd prefer—"

"Oh, no—no," she managed to stammer. "I'm all right, and you can sit down if you want."

He did, gracefully and without any hesitation. "My name is Ryan Davis," he said. "And if you're really all right, I have to tell you that your sundae is being flooded with something that looks like it could supply Niagara Falls."

"Oh. This is a banana split," Jill blurted out. "And I don't even like them."

Ryan Davis's eyes twinkled with amusement. "Well, that's a legitimate reason to cry, then."

Jill realized that she was staring at his face. Up close, it was even more compelling than she'd originally thought. He had little laugh lines around his eyes, and his beard framed a full, sensitive mouth. He was terribly handsome.

"Now I know who you are," Ryan said, snapping two fingers together. "You're in the psych one-oh-one class."

"And you're the T.A." Jill found, to her surprise, that she was smiling. Even through all those tears!

"You were there for the inkblot experiment this morning," Ryan remembered. "Is that what's the matter? Did the second film of all those disasters get you this depressed?"

Jill laughed, as he had intended her to. "Of course it did," she said. "The volcano wasn't bad enough, but when we went right into a nuclear holocaust, and then killed off the entire grasshopper population of the Southwest, that was more than I could bear."

He was grinning. "And so you felt you had to eat your way through a banana split just to compensate."

"Compensate," Jill repeated. "Compensation. Isn't that one of our coping mechanisms that we're learning about in psych?" Jill was interested now. She put down her spoon and leaned forward. "Isn't that when a person can't have what she wants, so she has to go out and find a substitute?"

"You've got it," Ryan said. "I guess you're one of Professor Blake's better students." He put his hand out and touched hers for a fraction of a moment, there on the table. "Are you feeling cheered up? Because you certainly seem to be."

"Oh, I'm much better. Now that I know I've been compensating, everything makes more sense to me." Jill found a tissue in her purse and wiped impatiently at the tears that still stained her face. "Definitely."

Ryan frowned slightly. "So you've been compensating. I guess you mean with the banana split—when you don't even like them?"

"Exactly. And not only that. Would you believe that I just signed up for the water polo club? That's not like me at all! But now I understand that I had to compensate in some way, so it's really okay."

"I see." Ryan was staring at her. "No, actually I don't see. Why don't we start at the beginning? You haven't told me your name yet."

Jill actually laughed. "I'm Jill Gardner."

"Ah-ha! The famous Jill Gardner who writes the *Voice* column? Weren't you supposed to have been responsible for the food fight and the protest demonstration?"

44

"Yes, that's me. Except that I never meant to start anything. I was just trying to write a humorous column."

Ryan put up a hand. "Hey, never apologize. You wrote a good piece, and it happened to get instant results from the students who have to eat that weird fare."

"You sound as though you're not one of them."

"I'm not. I don't live on campus."

Jill hadn't known that there were any Rosemont students who lived off campus. "You aren't a graduate student, are you?" she asked.

"Nope. I'm in my third year."

"But you look so—"

"Old? Maybe that's because I am old. And I feel even older than I look, believe me."

What a mysterious thing to say, Jill thought. But then there was a lot that seemed mysterious about this Ryan Davis. And all of it made her intensely curious.

Toni's words came back to her at that moment. "There's nothing like an older man, Jill." Well, Ryan Davis was an older man, all right. And what was more, Jill knew that he had a very strange effect on her. Just like the day of the psych experiment, she found her heart beating, and she was feeling totally mesmerized by his dark, compassionate eyes.

What do you think, Toni? Jill was stretching her silent plea across the miles to Seattle. *Is this somebody going to be my older man? This guy could help me forget about Craig, if only I could get his interest.*

And then, oddly, she could almost hear Toni's voice answering her back, "Go for it, Jill!"

"No more questions about me, please," Ryan said. "We're trying to find out what you're compensating for. You realize, don't you, that if you go on compensating like this—" he pointed to the banana split—"you'll end up weighing two hundred pounds?"

"Oh, no," Jill said. "Not with all that exercise I'm going to get playing water polo."

Ryan looked confused. "Run this by me again," he said. "You buy a banana split when you don't like them. So does this mean you're going to play water polo, even though you don't like it?"

"I don't know if I like it. I've never played it. Never even seen a game." There was a measure of pride in Jill's words.

Ryan's piercing gaze was like that of a scientist, studying a rare and exotic species.

"May I ask, what are we compensating *for*?" he finally asked. "No, wait—let me guess. It's about a boy, right?"

"That's right. Give the man a cigar." Jill no longer had the terrible pain in her heart, even when the subject of Craig was brought up. Instead, she felt her heart flutter a little, the way it usually did when she tried something new. And she was certainly in the mood for trying something different—as an experiment, maybe.

"Do you want to talk about your boyfriend?" Ryan asked.

"Thank you, but, no." Jill pushed away the banana split dish. "I think I can handle it. I'd rather just forget it—forget him—and get on with my life here at Rosemont."

Ryan was nodding. "Sounds like a good, sensible idea. Well—" He pushed his chair back as though he were getting ready to leave.

Please don't go now! she thought frantically.

Aloud, she said, "Ryan? I want to thank you. You've helped me a lot."

"I can't imagine how," he said sincerely. "But if you say so, then—I'm glad."

"I hope I can help you someday," Jill said quickly. She didn't want him to leave. "You were very kind to talk to me."

"What can I tell you?" He put out his hands in a helpless gesture. "I'm probably going to be the world's most famous psychologist someday—after Sigmund Freud, of course."

"Is that your major? Psychology?"

He nodded. "One of them. Marketing is the other. And it's a lot of hard work, believe me. That's why I have to get going now, Jill. Tons of homework. Papers to write. Research to do—"

Jill had a sudden inspiration. "You know, maybe *you* should join the water polo club, Ryan. It sounds like you need an outlet, with all that hard work you do."

She was being devious, of course. She wanted Ryan to be on the water polo team so she could see more of him. She was definitely attracted to this man!

"I don't think so," Ryan said. "It does sound like a fun sport, but much too time consuming for me."

He stood up and was ready to leave. "Take care, Jill. And I hope you solve your problems in some other way." He looked down at the melting banana split, smiled, and she noticed those neat laugh lines around his warm eyes. "That ice cream looks like a pretty soggy mess."

Before she could say a decent goodbye, he had turned and was heading out the door of the coffee shop.

SIX

Dear Toni,

First I'll tell you the bad news. Craig and I are now officially not a couple. I know you told me to break it to him gently, but guess what—he broke it to *me* gently! I was a basket case, Toni, as you can imagine. But I think I may have found a solution, and it's one that you would definitely approve of.

If that sounds mysterious, it could be because I've met someone who is mysterious—and handsome. And sensitive to problems. And older, Toni, oh, so very much older!

This wonderful human being is named Ryan Davis, and he's the teacher's assistant in my psych class. He has compelling eyes, a dark beard(!), and looks absolutely wonderful in anything he wears—especially brown. He's probably at least twenty-two, and something tells me he's full of mystery.

I don't think he's one of the usual rich Rosemont snobs. I could be wrong about that, but he lives off campus and I don't think he even has a car, because I saw him walking toward town the other day.

Oh, Toni, can you tell that I have a lot of major feelings about Ryan Davis? Maybe this is just an experiment, to see how I can relate to an older man. Or maybe it's just a way of getting over my hurt about Craig. After all, Ryan is about as different from Craig as anyone I can imagine! All I know is, I want to spend more time with this fantastic guy! I don't know how I'm going to go about getting his attention, but I certainly intend to *try*.

Wish me luck, Toni. Wish me luck.

In the meantime, there's the freshman I told you about, Terrence Lind. He pops up from nowhere at least four times a day and always has a big smile for me and lots of nice things to talk about. I really like Terrence. He's very likeable. But he's my age exactly. And there's something about him that I can't quite place—a feeling that I know him from some-where else, but I can't figure out where. It's bugging me.

Anyway, I think I've found out that you're absolutely right when you say there's nothing like an older man!

So how are things with you, Toni? I know it's only been a couple of days since we spoke, but it seems like an eternity with so much happening in my life.

Out of Love*

I don't know why I bother to ask you anything. You never write letters anyway. I know, I know, you're busy. But so am I.

In fact, when you hear from me next, I'll be an experienced sportswoman. Are you ready for this? I am on the water polo team! I'll tell you more about it after I've gone to my first practice.

Take good care of yourself, Toni. I worry about you being all on your own in that little apartment. I hope you aren't starving—are you? Okay, okay, I know that's a mom's line, but I am your best friend.

So long for now. Wish me luck in the pool—and on dry land, too.

Lotsa love, Jill

P.S. How was the egg mess?

Dear Jill,

Okay, I'm writing a letter on the exact same day that I got your letter. Are you satisfied?

You sure had plenty of news in your letter. And it all happened so fast. I'm not certain I was able to understand it all, but I think the gist of it was that you're working on a new love. And I say, good for you!

The guy in question sounds dreamy. A *beard*, no less. This sounds better than anyone

51

I've ever met, except for Brandt, of course. I wish I could get Brandt to grow a beard. As a theatrical director, he really should have one, don't you think?

Did I read your letter right? I thought you said you were going to play *water polo*. Now that's awesome. I am proud of you, Jill! Sounds like a terrific way to meet people and have some fun at the same time.

Things here in Seattle are never dull. Rehearsals are proceeding, without me, for *A Walk in the Dark*. That's the play that's set in the South. All about a genteel family and a creepy bride who marries into it. I'm helping the stage manager by doing props. Last night I handed the bride, who is supposed to shoot her husband, a gun with no blanks in it. After she pulled the trigger three or four times and nothing happened, the husband fell down anyway.

I yelled from backstage, "Oh, isn't that too bad—a heart attack at such an early age."

We had to stop rehearsal because we were all laughing so hard. I never said I could do props—I was only helping out.

Well, that's all for now, Jill. Take care of yourself. I worry about you as much as you worry about me.

Luv, luv, luv,
your best friend, Toni

P.S. I am not starving, *Mom*.

SEVEN

"And the quiz this week will be on Maslow's theory on the hierarchy of needs," Professor Blake was saying to Jill's psych class. "You will read the chapter, please, and familiarize yourselves with the steps that lead to the self-actualization of an individual."

Jill, who was always a good student, found that she was not concentrating at all on Professor Blake's lecture. In fact, her notes looked like a jumble that a high school freshman might have written—especially the heart she had drawn. It had lace all around its edge and "Ryan and Jill" penciled inside it!

Ryan was seated in the corner of the classroom, up front near the blackboard. That day Jill was spending all her time stealing glances at him, remembering how wonderful he had been to talk with that night in the coffee shop. She wondered if every other girl in the room noticed his eyes, too. They were so bright and intelligent and full of that mystery that she always sensed.

Anyway, she thought dismally, Ryan was certainly not looking her way, and he'd made no attempt to talk with her since that night five days ago. She was beginning to think he never would, unless he found her weeping into a banana split again—and she couldn't go around doing that every night!

Now, as the class was ending, she decided to be bold and go up to him. "Nothing ventured, nothing gained," her mother often said to her. *So, here goes,* Jill thought.

"Hi, Ryan," she said brightly, stepping in front of him as he was about to leave the classroom.

"Oh, hi, Jill." He looked sort of glad to see her, anyway. But he also looked as though he was in a rush to get somewhere.

"I won't keep you or anything," Jill said quickly as she managed to fall into step beside him as he started out the door and down the hall of the psych building.

"That's good, because honestly I have a pressing problem that I have to go and solve."

"Oh, I'm sorry to hear that." Jill found that she almost had to run to keep up with his firm, powerful stride. "Anything I can help with?" she puffed.

Ryan grinned and kept walking. "Not unless you're a crackerjack typist. That's what I'm searching for, a good typist to do an advanced psych paper. I've already tried all the typists' ads on the bulletin boards, and everybody's booked up. I need it yesterday."

Jill felt a stab of disappointment at herself. "I'm sorry, but I'm not much of a typist. I wish I were. In fact, I write all my columns in longhand and turn them over to Russel, the newspaper editor, for typing." That gave her an idea. "Hey, maybe you could ask Russel if he'd type it for you, or if he knows of anyone else who could."

Ryan looked grateful. "Thanks, Jill. I never thought of the Rosemont *Voice* office. Of course! I'll do that. At this point I'll be glad to pay anything to get that paper neatly typed. Not that I can afford much, but—"

Jill tried to think of a way she could help. Then she remembered the copy shop. "Listen, I get a discount on all copying because I work nights at the campus print shop. If you need to have your paper copied, just come over there and I'll Xerox it for you. Wholesale rates."

"I'd really appreciate that, if it wouldn't get you into trouble."

"Oh, no, not at all. Mr. Allen is always telling me to take advantage of the discount rate."

They had gone outside, and Ryan stopped walking for a moment to look down at Jill. "What a sweet kid you are. I hope you're feeling happier now—"

"Yes, I am, I—"

"But, listen, I really have to run right now. I'll see you at the copy shop one of these nights."

"Sure—" Jill started to say, but Ryan was so quick that he had disappeared around the corner of the fine arts building by the time she could continue.

So that's all I am—"*a sweet kid,*" she thought. And here she'd gone to such trouble to wear her prettiest pink blouse and soft gray wool skirt that day. She might as well have worn a baby bonnet and diapers, for all Ryan noticed.

Let's face it, she thought. *I am a kid to him. And unless I find a way to make him notice me, I'll always be just a kid to him!*

"Hey, kid, how are you doing?" called out Terrence Lind, catching up with her on the path and flashing his engaging grin. He was much taller than Ryan, and he certainly looked wholesome, like one of those athletes on a Wheaties box. Terrence was all sunshine and good cheer, not like the dark and unreachable Ryan.

"Hi, Terrence," she said flatly.

"I wanted to tell you, I read your column on hometown romances last week. It was great. I read your column and Jake's column word for word."

"I hope you're not putting me in a class with him. He's a *genius*."

"So are you, in your own way. Jill, that column was not only funny it was—poignant. I mean, it sounded like you wrote it from the heart."

"I did." Jill kicked at a tuft of grass along the path. "I was very involved in a hometown romance, as I think I told you."

"Was? Past tense?"

She squinted into the sunlight to look up at Terrence. "Past tense," she said. "Craig and I broke up last week."

"And it's final?"

"Yes. Final for the next four years, anyway. But Terrence, I don't want to—"

"I know. You don't want to talk about it. I don't blame you. You know what you ought to do? Come with me after supper and drown your sorrows in a big bowl of ice cream."

Jill couldn't help it, she started laughing out loud.

"Oh, Terrence, I'm not laughing at you," she explained. "It's just that—well, that's exactly what I did try to do when Craig called me that night."

"Oh? I'm sorry I wasn't around."

I'm not, Jill thought. *I had Ryan Davis to console me.*

"It's nice of you to suggest that," she said. "But I don't think I'll be interested in ice cream until my next big crisis. And maybe not even then!"

"Okay." Terrence looked somewhat subdued. "I suppose there's no point in asking you to have coffee with me later, either?"

He was asking her for a date, Jill realized. Or at least he was trying, in a subtle way, to find out if she was interested in going out with him.

"That's kind of you, Terrence, but in just about a half hour I'm due at practice. I've taken up a sport."

"A sport." He looked bemused. "Am I supposed to guess which one? Is it field hockey?" She shook her head. "Cross country? No? Soccer—no, I'll bet it's not soccer."

"You'd never guess in a million years. Water polo!"

Now it was Terrence's turn to laugh out loud.

"You're right, I'd never have guessed in a million years. Well, it ought to give you something funny to write about in your next column."

"Hey, I never thought of that. Maybe it will."

Terrence was staring at her in a thoughtful way. "Jill, I guess you know that I'd like to be your friend. But I don't want to be pushy or rush you into anything. If you ever feel like having coffee with me, or dinner, or seeing a movie in town, or whatever—will you let me know?"

She was moved to silence. "Why—yes. Of course, I will." *What a good guy he is,* she thought, *to realize that I might need time to get over my breakup with Craig.*

This boy is a gem, Jill thought, looking at him with new eyes and seeing a very good-looking guy. *He'd be perfect for somebody—even somebody like me, if I hadn't already gone and fallen for a certain T.A. with a beard and a sexy voice.*

"You're a good friend, Terrence," she said warmly, giving him a pat on the arm. He gave her a funny look when she touched him, and she wondered if he had a crush on her.

58

Maybe "You're a good friend" had been the wrong thing to say.

That amounted to just about what Ryan had said to her. "What a sweet kid you are."

EIGHT

"You're not really going through with it, are you, Jill?" Cassandra was stretched out on her bed with a book in one hand and Jelly Bean, her cat, curled up in a ball beside her.

"Sure I am." Jill had just changed into her blue Speedo bathing suit, and she struck a dramatic pose with her hand on her hip, as if for an old-fashioned swim wear ad. "How's this? Do I look like one of those California beach girls, or what?"

"No, but that's not the point. You're supposed to look like an aquatic athlete, right? And with that plain racing suit you do, Jill. You look impressively athletic. Like a member of the U.S. Olympic team, at least."

"Great. Because I don't feel that way. I feel like someone who hasn't worked out in the water for a long, long time."

"That's the way the old cookie crumbles," Cassandra said, smiling. It was a joke, because Cassandra thought all clichés were silly and obnoxious.

"Well, anyway, I'd better get on over there and see what this game is all about." Jill started nervously rummaging around the room for her beach towel.

"I think you're crazy," Cassandra said in a singsong voice. "You wouldn't catch me flopping around in a pool like that with a bunch of water freaks."

"You never know, Cassie." Jill shook her finger as if giving a lecture. "Have you ever heard of *this* saying: 'When life hands you a lemon, make lemonade'?"

Cassandra stared at her roommate as though Jill were a candidate for the funny farm.

"Is that a statement with some kind of deep philosophical meaning, Miss Gardner?"

"Yes, in a way. It all has to do with compensation, which we're learning about in psych. You must have learned it, too," Jill answered.

"Maybe I wasn't in class that day." Cassie stretched lazily, and her long black hair fell down like a curtain over the cat.

"You should go to class more often, Cassie," Jill scolded. "Well, compensation is the reason I'm going to play water polo. Because I still feel empty about the breakup with Craig, and I was feeling like a very wishy-washy person, and—"

"I know, Jill," Cassandra said, nodding. "I understand, really I do. And you're probably doing the right thing—for you. So why don't you just go on and make your lemonade, and I'll probably see you later. Oh, and—good luck!"

"Thanks. I'll probably need it." Jill threw on a pair of sweatpants and a matching sweatshirt, slipped into a jacket, and headed out the door, the towel tossed over her shoulder.

She was halfway to the field house when she began to get cold feet.

"Why am I doing this?" she asked herself out loud. "I don't need an extra activity. I've got more than enough to keep me busy here at Rosemont. And besides, it has been a long time since the eighth grade swim team."

But she kept going because she had signed her name to that club sheet. If nothing else, she'd keep her word and give this sport a try. And after all, she had completed her senior lifesaving exam. So she couldn't be *too* much out of condition, could she?

Cautious old Jill is on her way to something brand-new, she kept reciting to herself, almost as a litany. Breaking out of the old mold! Coming out of her shell!

The words had a familiar ring to them. Hadn't she said almost the same thing just last month when she went to that rich boy's party with Kyle Robertson? She'd had a terrible time and had learned that—for her, at least—friendships should not be rushed into. "You have to find people like yourself," Cassie had told her, quite wisely, when Jill was moaning about knowing so few students at Rosemont.

Well, she already *had* met some people like herself, through the newspaper and the copy shop, and some very nice people right in her dorm. So why was she heading toward a bunch of athletes who played water polo?

The field house was a long, old building that looked like a Quonset hut left over from the Second World War. Jill hadn't even been inside yet, except for one quick tour at the beginning of the year. But now, as she walked into a huge basketball arena, she remembered the smells: sweat and old socks and floor wax. Just like the gym back home in Seattle, but even more so.

She found her way to the pool by following the scent of chlorine. The smell grew stronger as she walked, and finally she saw a makeshift sign with an arrow saying "Water Polo Club—11 A.M. every day."

A boy gave her a combination lock after she showed her campus ID card, and she went to the girls' locker room to leave her clothes, folded neatly, in a locker.

It's now or never, she told herself sternly and threw open one of the double doors that led to the pool. A chorus of cheers greeted her.

"Hey! There's our new member. I told you she'd show up," yelled one of the heads bobbing in the water. They looked alike, because they were all wearing weird-looking, tight bathing caps in either red or blue. "Hi, Jill. Glad you could make it," they chorused.

63

A short, stocky boy with thick glasses, dressed in his street clothes, came marching over to her.

"Hello," he said shortly, sounding like an army drill sergeant. "My name is Malcolm, and I'm the president of this club. I warn you right now, I take this game very seriously."

She felt him staring at her through his Coke-bottle glasses, and she squirmed. Was he examining her biceps, and deciding that she was too scrawny for this game? Jill swallowed and almost felt like apologizing for being there at all.

"H-hello, Malcolm," she managed to say.

He didn't crack a smile. "First, let me see those toenails," he commanded.

"What? Did you say toenails?"

"Well, of course," Malcolm replied impatiently. "What kind of players do you think we are? Dirty ones?"

"No, of course not. And my toenails are never dirty."

Malcolm bent down to examine her feet. *Is he for real?* she thought.

"I don't mean dirty toenails. I mean *long* toenails, for heaven's sake. If players have long toenails, then they have a real weapon to use underwater, where the refs can't see. They can scratch their opponents and do serious damage with their toenails." Malcolm looked up at her sternly. "That would be playing dirty!"

Jill started laughing, mostly out of nervousness. "I get it now. Well, as you can see, my nails are clipped nice and short—with no lethal ragged edges."

"Yes." Malcolm cleared his throat importantly. "So, let's get you into a bathing cap and into the water—see what you can do."

At that point Jill felt like running away and never coming back, but something—a streak of stubbornness—made her accept the red bathing cap and head for the pool. Besides, the water looked inviting. The smell of chlorine was very strong, and the noise level was pretty high, with all the players splashing around.

As she forced her hair into the tight cap, she thought that it all looked pretty exciting to someone who hadn't been doing much except study and write.

The minute she got into the pool, three players swam over to greet her. "We want to tell you 'Rule Number One,'" a boy whispered.

"Above all, do *not* pay any attention to Malcolm," said one of the girls. "None of us do. He thinks he's some kind of superexecutive, but all he is is the president, and we only elected him because no one else wanted the job. Besides, the only stroke Malcolm can do is the doggie paddle."

"Yeah, he's totally obnoxious," said Paul, the boy she remembered as captain of the team. "Just take him with a grain of salt—a big one."

Whew! That was a big relief to Jill. As long as everyone wasn't going to be like Malcolm the Terrible, maybe she'd stand a chance at water polo.

"Um—what do I do, anyway?" she asked Paul.

"You learn to swim without hands, like this—you see? Just practice keeping afloat. Right now we're finishing up fifteen minutes of the eggbeater kick. That's so you can keep your hands free for catching the ball." Someone threw the ball over their way, and Paul demonstrated how he twirled it in the palm of one hand, controlling it before he sent it on its way to another player.

"You see? Nothing to it. And the object, of course, is to get the ball into the opponent's goal—with hand, foot, or head."

"Hand, foot, or head," Jill repeated with trepidation. "And those cage things on each end are the goals?"

"Yes, something like hockey. Now, you're wearing a red cap today, so you're on the red team for practice. Those of us in blue caps are the opposing team."

"Do you think you're finally ready now, Gardner?" Malcolm growled from the platform beside the pool.

"Remember—try to ignore him," whispered Paul as he swam off.

Malcolm blew a shrill whistle, so loud that it made Jill almost leap out of the water. She had always been sensitive to loud noises.

After the eggbeater kick came another form of torture: a thousand yards of the butterfly. Jill was exhausted and panting in no time at all.

"I thought I was in semidecent shape," she said to Paul, feeling ashamed. "I figured I could hack this because I've had swimming experience, but—" She was puffing too much to finish.

"Don't get discouraged," Paul said kindly. "Polo practice was a shock to all of us, at first. Really. Every one of us was ready to give up in the beginning."

"Really?"

"Yeah. But you're a good swimmer, Jill. The endurance will come in time. It really will."

That made her feel somewhat better, but she was still bushed. She was treading water because the pool was deep. In fact, it seemed to be over their heads at all points. Since it was taking all her energy just to stay afloat, she wondered what she'd ever do if the ball came near her.

And then it did, not too long after a practice whistle blew.

"Catch it!" yelled someone on the red team. "No, hit it!" "Hey, pass it along this way."

Spluttering and struggling, Jill managed to leap out of the water—sort of like a wimpy dolphin, she thought—and make a swipe at the ball. But it flew right past her, and she went flopping back down, sinking deep below the water.

"Good try, anyway," a red-capped girl called out.

But Jill was humiliated and discouraged. The game was *hard*. Here she was huffing and out of breath already, and she'd only just begun. Would she ever be able to command the ball the way these kids did?

"No, no, *no*," Malcolm was complaining to the whole group in his military voice. "None of you are taking this game seriously. You're all just clowning around!"

"No, we're not, Mal baby," yelled someone on the blue team, and all of a sudden, in swift and perfect precision, everyone on that team disappeared below the surface of the water. It was so neatly timed that Jill had to laugh, but quietly, as she saw Malcolm sputtering with indignation.

"I never—what is the *use*, anyway?" Malcolm declared. "What kind of a group *is* this? Do any of you realize that we're playing against Morris College in just one week's time?"

"We'll be ready, Malcolm," called out the red team, and Jill heard someone counting off quietly. "Three, two, one, go!" and the entire red team dove under the water. Jill decided that she'd better join them, so she went down, too.

It was beautiful under there. She opened her eyes wide and looked around, enchanted by sparkling silver blue water and the millions of tiny bubbles, almost like champagne bubbles, that swirled around each diver.

This is fantastic, Jill thought. *I love it*. The exercise felt great, she realized, and being with such a zany group of kids was exactly the right prescription for a girl who'd had to say goodbye to her hometown love.

"It seems to me that there's just no point to this," Malcolm was saying when all the players came back up for air. He looked as though he'd been mortally wounded.

"Malcolm, why don't you relax?" Paul said to him. "We know our stuff. We'll cream Morris College, or any other school you schedule us against."

"Yeah, Malcolm, give us a break!"

"Be a sport, Mal. We're here every single day, you know. We have to let off some steam!"

Jill loved their attitude. She had a feeling that they were pretty decent players, but, as they said, they had to "let off steam" at times. And it didn't seem to her like such a bad idea.

"Okay, now," Paul finally told the club. "Let's play ball."

From then on, the practice went smoothly, with everyone in his or her assigned place and the ball zinging around swiftly, propelled by sure, deft passes. Jill had a chance at the ball several times, and once—only once—did she distinguish herself by catching it and sending it off to a red player. And in the right direction!

That encouraged her, a little bit. And a little bit was all she needed.

Just before the practice came to an end, she looked up and saw a lone figure watching from the door. It was Ryan Davis. Her heart leaped. Maybe Ryan had taken her suggestion and he was here to see about joining the club!

But unfortunately Malcolm got to him first.

After a few minutes of listening to Malcolm, Ryan's face changed completely. He frowned as though he had just stumbled into a mental institution and looked as though he were trying to find his way out—fast.

Oh, Malcolm, don't blow it, Jill implored silently, but she knew that it was too late.

"I could kill that Malcolm," she muttered out loud, and one of the girls, Suzie, overheard her.

"You'll have to stand in line first. But why?"

"Just look—he's scaring away a possible new member. And it's someone that I—that I wish would join!"

"Mal does that all the time," Suzie said. "Sometimes we think we ought to keep him on a leash. Or maybe we should put a sign by the door saying, 'Beware of Malcolm: he bites.' Anyway, I'm sorry that Malcolm scared away your boyfriend."

Jill felt an odd sensation. *Your boyfriend*, Suzie had said.

Oh, how she wished Ryan Davis really was her boyfriend!

NINE

Dear Toni,

It was great—the water polo, I mean. I felt as though I fitted right in, even though I'm a pathetic player right now.

And all that swimming is really beneficial. I found that my mind was clearer than ever, afterward, and I wrote a really inspired paper on *Macbeth* for English class.

Toni, I can't believe what you said about the heart attack. If only I could have been there.

I told Cassie about it, and she said that you must be a first-rate loony. She meant it as a sincere compliment! But, of course, I've told you what Cassie is like—a strange bird herself. What worries me most about her is that she's sort of negative about college, most of the time.

I mean, it's *great* to be self-sufficient, and I admire her for being an ". . . island unto itself"—but I wish she'd make a few friends. That's what college is for. So far, I'm practically her only friend, and even I don't see much of her. She's always taking long walks all by herself, or else has her nose in a book. Real heavy stuff, too.

I wish you could get up here for another visit and meet her someday. You'll see that she's a huge improvement over Sheridan. I guess I'll always have you to thank for getting me out of *that* mess! Who else but you could manage to spill an entire jar of fancy bubble bath in my hateful ex-roommate's bathtub? Sheridan sure did look funny with nothing showing over those bubbles but her nose, didn't she?"

Well, I've rambled on long enough. But I do have something to ask you, Toni. You're always telling me to date older guys. So—*help*! How do I make this guy Ryan notice me? I see him often enough, but he thinks I'm a kid. I remember you had the same problem with Brandt, but you managed to get yourself stuck in an elevator with him—as only you could do!—and then he began to realize how cute you really are.

I don't know how to find an ancient elevator to get stuck in with Ryan. So what do I do next? Answer, please.

All my love, Jill

But it would be a while before she'd get a reply from Toni. So Jill knew, deep down, that she would have to come up with her own solution. That was why she was delighted when, that night at the copy shop, one of the customers who came in was Ryan Davis.

She was busy doing some priority filing for Mr. Allen and didn't notice at first that he had walked in. But when she looked up, there he was—Ryan, in person. Immediately her heart began to beat faster, and she hoped she didn't look too flustered. She hurried over to the counter that separated the print shop from the customers.

"Ryan. Hello," she said, trying to sound casual. After all, if she acted too eager, she thought, she'd seem even more like an eighteen-year-old kid to him.

"Hi, Jill. So you *do* work here. I thought maybe you actually spent your evenings eating banana splits." He was smiling warmly, and the sight of that amused face made her feel weak all over.

"Please, don't remind me of that gross ice-cream pig-out," she said. "I never finished it, you know."

"Of course not. But you have recovered from the crisis of the boyfriend?"

He must be interested, Jill thought hopefully. *He wouldn't ask about my boyfriend if he weren't a little bit interested.*

"Pretty much. And a member in good standing of the water polo club, in addition. And by the way—"

"I know. You saw me at the pool a couple of mornings ago." Ryan shook his head darkly. "That bozo who runs the club is some character."

"But that's what I wanted to tell you. You shouldn't let Malcolm scare you away, if you want to play water polo, because no one pays any attention to him. They're a great bunch of kids—really!"

Ryan put his manuscript folder down on the counter. "Well, I wasn't planning to join, Jill. I was just looking in to see what the game looked like since I happened to be in the field house. But I really don't have time for games." He looked at Jill in a wistful sort of way. "I wish I did, sometimes."

"Oh," Jill said. She was completely at a loss for words.

He changed the subject. "Anyway, I'm here because I need my advanced psych paper copied. As you can see, I was able to get a typist. One of the typists from the *Voice* did do it—and fast." His eyes flickered with gratitude. "Thanks to your suggestion, Jill."

Her knees felt suddenly weak. "I'm glad, Ryan." She just *loved* saying his name. *Uh, oh, you've developed a major crush here, Jill,* she told herself.

"I can copy your paper for you right away," she told him, mentally deciding that Mr. Allen's big filing job could wait—even if she had to work overtime later on. "And I will be able to get you the discount rate."

"Fine." Ryan showed her the paper, which was about twenty-two pages of technical psych theory.

"Jill," Mr. Allen called out. "Don't neglect that filing, please. It's very important."

"Maybe I should come back for my paper later," Ryan said.

"Um, yes, maybe you're right. We close around nine-thirty, depending on how busy we are."

"Good. I'll be studying at the library until then." He pretended to tip an imaginary hat toward Jill. "Thanks again." And he left.

"More copying?" Mr. Allen said, coming from the back room. "I guess we're getting into that crazy busy season when all the students are doing term papers. Sometimes I wonder—"

"I know, Mr. Allen," Jill said, teasing him. "You've said it many times before. Sometimes you wonder why you don't open a nice, sensible print shop in town, instead of dealing with all these nutty college kids!"

"You said it," Mr. Allen grumbled and went back to his work in the next room.

Later, as Jill was feeding Ryan's paper through the copy machine, she had a brilliant idea. In fact, it was the kind of thing that Toni would have told her to do, if Toni had been there to whisper in her ear.

"I'll keep a page of his paper out," she whispered out loud to no one but herself. "Then I'll have an excuse to go and find him, and we'll have another chance to talk."

She had never been a schemer, but drastic measures were often called for in drastic situations, she thought. Ryan was just too hard to pin down. Why was that, anyway?

She managed to hide page ten of his report, and to insert two pages numbered eleven instead. *Jill, I'm proud of you,* she could hear Toni saying somewhere in the recesses of her mind. *You're using the old noodle, for a change.*

Ryan came back at exactly nine-thirty, as Mr. Allen was getting ready close up the shop. He paid his bill and watched as Jill slipped into her jacket.

"It's kind of dark out there," Ryan said. "Do you walk down to your dorm all alone at night?"

"Yes, usually. But there are plenty of people around at this hour and lots of lights along the way." Jill hesitated. "Of course it is kind of scary, sometimes, with all the shadows—"

Mr. Allen overheard this exchange. "You might as well walk the girl home, young man," he said. "Then we'll all feel assured that she's safe and secure."

"I think you're right, sir," Ryan said, smiling.

Jill's heart took a flying leap. Ryan was going to walk her to her dorm! She could hardly believe it.

"Good night, Mr. Allen," she called out as she and Ryan fell into step along the campus path. Ryan wasn't close to her, in a physical sense, but she felt his presence in a comforting sort of way.

The night *was* dark, with no moon, and the air was crisp and chilly. Their feet shuffled through fallen leaves, making a soft swish—a sound that contrasted with the silence between them. *This is all wrong*, she thought in a panic. *I've got to think of something to say.*

"So—how do you like being a T.A.?" she asked lamely.

"Oh, fine. Gives me that extra credit."

Silence again. She racked her brain to think of something intelligent to say.

"What do *you* think of Maslow's theory," she began, "on the, er—hierarchy of realization?"

"That's the hierarchy of *needs*, Jill," Ryan said kindly. "And to tell you the truth, I don't do much thinking about it. I guess I'm just too busy to do much analyzing these days."

She felt foolish. "I guess you must be busy. I mean, you always sound so terribly busy—"

"Look, Jill, please forgive me for saying this. It's kind of hard for me to make a lot of small talk right now. I didn't get a wink of sleep last night, and my mind isn't functioning all that well. I pulled an all-nighter to study for an exam."

"Oh. I'm sorry—of course, we don't have to talk." Jill fell into a silence, too, and they strolled comfortably along. Suddenly, though, it seemed to Jill that everywhere she looked there were couples locked in tight embraces—on the benches, under trees, and in the shadows of bushes.

It looks as though the world is full of lovers tonight, Jill thought. *And here I am strolling along with a man who's too tired even to talk. And too old for me. Or at least he thinks he is.* A sadness descended on Jill that she couldn't identify.

Just before they reached the lighted area in front of McGregor Hall, a tall figure stepped out from under a tree, as though he'd been waiting there. It was Terrence.

"Hi, Jill," he said eagerly. "I came by to tell you some good news—oh. Hi there, Ryan."

"Hi," Ryan said, obviously not knowing who Terrence was.

"I know you from Professor Blake's psych class," Terrence explained. He looked utterly amazed to see Jill walking along with Ryan in the dark. But, to his credit, he didn't say anything dumb.

"Well," Ryan said abruptly. "I see you're in good hands now, Jill, so I'll say so long. And, thanks again—for the copying."

"You're welcome," she said. She watched Ryan striding off down the road past the many rhododendron bushes that led to the front gate of the college, where stone lions stood guard.

"Guess I interrupted something, didn't I?" Terrence sounded apologetic.

"No, of course not." Jill turned back and flashed him a big smile. "Ryan is—you know, just a sort of friend."

"Is he?" Terrence had been watching her as her eyes followed Ryan the whole way. "Well, that's good. He is sort of old."

"Right, I know." Jill was absolutely bursting with feelings of sadness and disappointment. *Darn you, Terrence!* she thought. *If you hadn't been standing*

*here, I might just have been able to get Ryan to kiss me—
even if it was just a kiss on the cheek.*

I wouldn't have been content with a kiss on the cheek,
she realized suddenly. *I would have wanted a real kiss,
so I could know what his beard feels like, up close.*

She was glad that it was too dark for Terrence to
see the telltale blush that colored her cheeks right
then.

"What's your news?" she asked Terrence.

"Oh. I took your advice and went to see Russel,
at the *Voice*, and he's agreed to let me write a news
story or two. And guess what? He assigned me to go
with the water polo club when they go to play
Morris College."

"That's wonderful, Terrence." Jill meant it
sincerely.

"I know you were probably planning to write
about the club yourself, but this will be different,"
Terrence explained. "You'll be writing yours humorously, and mine will be straight sports reporting.
I'm really excited about it."

"I don't blame you. It's a good way to get
started." Jill tore her eyes away from the now-empty
road and looked up into Terrence's happy green
eyes. "Who knows, maybe someday you'll be a
famous campus writer like Jake Randall. And I'll be
able to say I knew you when!"

"Oh, sure." Terrence seemed sort of quiet then.
"Well, I guess I won't bother you anymore, Jill. You
probably have studying to do, after working all
evening."

"Oh, yes, I do. Of course."

"Good night, then."

"Good night, Terrence. Take care."

As she went up the porch steps of McGregor, Jill remembered that she was carrying, in her own folder, page ten of Ryan's manuscript. She was going to have to find some way to return it to him—pretty fast.

TEN

Ryan wasn't in psych class the next day, but Jill didn't intend to let that stop her. After all, she had to return his missing paper, didn't she?

She went up to Professor Blake after the class was over.

"I'm sorry to bother you, sir," she said. "But I have a paper that belongs to your teacher's assistant, and I wonder if you might know his address?"

Professor Blake looked at her suspiciously. "You sure you're not one of those girls who gets a crush on my assistant every single semester?"

"Oh, no, sir," Jill said with a straight face. "As you can see, I have page ten of his report, and he'll be needing it. I work at the copy shop on campus, you see, and—"

"Oh, very well," Professor Blake interrupted her. "I think I know you already, anyway. Jill Gardner. A good student. A levelheaded young lady. I guess there won't be any harm in giving you Ryan's address."

So saying, he scribbled an address on a small sheet of notepaper and gave it to her. Then he turned to another student who was waiting to ask a question.

Jill clutched the piece of paper as though it were gold plated. She might as well give it a shot right then, she thought. See if Ryan was home, wherever home was. She was wearing her most comfortable flat walking shoes and didn't have another class for two hours. So she set out for town and actually whistled a little tune.

The town wasn't far at all, and Jill enjoyed the walk. When she reached Main Street, she asked a policeman directing traffic which way to go.

"State Avenue? Runs parallel to Main," the officer told her. "Just take any one of these side streets. I think that address—number eight-fifteen—would be off to your right as you hit State."

Jill followed his instructions and soon found herself standing outside a large, dark brown, wooden Victorian house. Probably it had been, at one time, a fine home, but now it had fallen into disrepair. Someone had obviously divided the house into many small apartments, as evidenced by the ten or so mailboxes that lined its sagging front porch.

"Oh, this is awful," she whispered at first, then remembered that the place where Toni lived wasn't much better. And really it didn't matter to students because they were so involved in their daily lives that wherever they slept at night just wasn't that important.

She found his name on one of the mailboxes: "Davis, R. Apt. 2A." She smiled slightly as she went inside to look for apartment 2A. The hall was old and smelled musty, with curls of dust gathered in the corners on the shabby linoleum floor. Jill went up the front stairs, guessing that any apartment labeled 2A would be on the second floor.

She was right. She found a battered door, sandwiched between two other doors, that was marked 2A with the name "Davis, R."

She knocked without hesitating. After all, she was there for a legitimate reason.

"Just a sec," Ryan's voice called out, and her stomach suddenly became full of knots.

The door swung open. Ryan stood there in jeans and a shirt in bare feet, and he didn't even look surprised to see her.

"Oh, Jill, am I glad you came. I'll bet you found my missing page ten?"

"Yes," Jill began, but he kept right on talking.

"I *am* glad you're here, and not just for that."

"You are?" she said happily.

"Yes! I'm having a wrestling match with a window shade. Can't make it go up or down. Do you know about things like window shades?"

"Um—oh, sure." Jill had never maneuvered a window shade in her life—her family had venetian blinds at home—but she was game to try anything if it meant being closer to Ryan.

He waved for her to come in, as though he were determined to solve the window shade problem before moving on to anything else. "Look at this thing—" He held up the pulled-out shade, and Jill thought he resembled a small boy, befuddled by a mechanical toy. Her heart went out to him.

"Let me see," she said gently. "I do sort of remember that my grandmother had a lot of shades like this, and as I recall she used to fix them with a fork."

"A fork? Great! I'll get you a fork." Ryan disappeared into the area that she assumed was the kitchen.

She took a quick look around. The entire apartment consisted of two small rooms—the sitting room she was in that was also a bedroom and the kitchen beyond that door. Maybe there was a bathroom somewhere. But, otherwise, that was it.

Not only was the apartment small, but it was also pathetically sloppy. But Jill could understand why. Everywhere she looked, on every single surface—chairs, tables, the bed—were open books. Ryan was knee-deep in his studies, that was obvious.

And he seemed so alone to her, so pitifully alone, as compared to the students who lived together in dorms.

He returned with the fork. "We're in luck, Jill. This is the last clean fork!"

"I'll try this winding method," Jill said. "But I can't really promise anything."

"I'm sure you can do it," he said.

So she was completely humiliated when, after she had turned and turned the roller with the fork tines, just the way her grandmother had done, the whole spring snapped and the shade went flying out of her hands. It landed on Ryan's bed, scattering his papers and pencils all over the floor.

"Oh, no, I'm afraid I've ruined it," Jill blurted out. "I'm so sorry—"

"Forget it. It's not mine. The landlord will have to get a new one, I suppose—eventually."

Jill felt utterly stupid and klutzy. The least she could do was pick up his papers and other things. She had just begun when Ryan stopped her.

"That's okay. It's not really important," Ryan said. "Did you say you have that missing page from my report, Jill?"

"Oh, yes, here it is."

"Thanks a million. You're a lifesaver." He glanced at it, then looked at her with interest. "That was very good of you to bring it all the way here, into town, for me."

She felt like the worst sort of deceitful female. "Well—after all—I knew you would be needing it."

"But you walked all this way. And on a chilly day, too."

"It's not that chilly. It's a beautiful autumn day. No rain for a change—" She was babbling because he was looking at her so intently.

"Look, I'd make you a cup of coffee, Jill, but I'm in the middle of so much studying that I can't stop. Big exam this afternoon."

"I never knew anyone who took studying as seriously as you do," Jill commented. "I'll make a cup of coffee for *you,* if that's all right. And then I'll be on my way. I can see how busy you are."

"Mmmm. Okay. Make one for yourself, too, please." Ryan had already picked up one of the books that was lying open on a chair.

Jill groped around in the dark, windowless kitchen, finally found a light switch, and actually shuddered. What a mess! But she put on a kettle of water to boil. Actually there was no kettle, only a saucepan, and it looked pretty darkened by countless boilings of water. She shook her head as she looked around the pathetic little space.

This place needs my touch, Jill thought, with deep maternal feelings washing over her. She wished she could clean both rooms for Ryan, cook some meals for him—

But she warned herself not to be pushy. She'd gone far enough, just to visit him—this time. She wasn't going to take another step soon.

"Here's coffee, Ryan," she said after locating two mugs and the tiny jar of instant in a grimy cupboard. The coffee, a quart of milk, and a box of Rice Krispies were the only items of food in the whole kitchen.

What a variety of dishes he must be able to concoct, Jill thought ironically. But the barrenness of this bachelor apartment was tearing at her heartstrings.

Ryan put his book down and came to the kitchen table. "Thanks, Jill. You're being awfully nice to me."

"Well, you were kind to me, the night of the banana split—remember?"

"Oh, yeah." He was still immersed in whatever he'd been studying, she realized. They both sat at the rickety kitchen table, and she could see him making an effort to concentrate on his guest.

"Ryan—why do you live here instead of in a dorm? If you don't mind my asking?"

"Isn't that obvious? I'm too old to be in a dorm, with a bunch of kids. And I work too hard—much too hard, to put up with all that noise."

"But, how old *are* you?"

"I'm twenty-two," he said. "But as I told you, I feel more like thirty."

"Why?"

He sipped at his coffee, then gazed thoughtfully into his steaming cup. "You want to know why? Because when I came to Rosemont the first time, years ago, I was a big party guy. A real playboy. Always having fun, never cracking the books."

"Oh," Jill said, beginning to understand. "You—did you fail?"

"Yep. 'Flunked out' is the brutal term." He leaned back and raised his arms over his head as though he needed a good stretch. "Stupid, wasn't it? My parents were paying my way, then, and I had it made. Except that I really messed up."

"How terrible." Jill felt sorry for him as she never had for anyone before.

"My own fault. My parents were furious. They're both ambitious, successful career types. They couldn't tolerate the thought of their only son being lazy. They didn't even speak to me for a year."

"That must have been awful for you," Jill guessed. "So now they won't pay for your schooling?"

"I wouldn't ask them to. They have my sisters to put through college now. No, I have to do this all on my own—for my self-esteem. So. I've been working at two and three jobs for the past couple of years and taking night courses. I managed to save up enough money to pay for a few semesters—to prove myself."

"You must be doing well now."

"Yeah, I am. I made dean's list last semester. That's how I was able to land the T.A. position." He sipped his coffee. "But I have to keep doing well in order to stay off academic probation. And I will get scholarships if I keep up the grades. That's why I spend every minute with the books. Every minute."

"I do admire you for that," Jill said.

He frowned. "No, don't. I was stupid the first time around, and now I've got to make up for it. Maybe I'm trying to compensate, just like you with your banana split!"

They both grinned. Jill felt very close to Ryan. Now only if he would let her clean his apartment, maybe, or cook a meal for him—

But she wasn't going to get that chance.

Out of Love

"Sorry, but as much as I enjoy having you here, I'm going to have to kick you out," Ryan said firmly, pushing back his chair. "You finished with your coffee? Good. I'm sorry, Jill, but I have some intense work ahead of me. That test today."

Jill took the hint—not too subtle—and put on her jacket. "Sorry to have kept you away from your work," she said.

"No problem. And thanks, Jill, for bringing page ten to me. You're a good friend—and I don't have many friends at school."

"Well, it seemed like the least I could do—" And she felt herself literally being pushed out of the apartment door.

Serves me right, she thought. She'd gone there under false pretenses, and she'd gotten kicked right out. But she'd ended up learning a great deal about Ryan. And none of it had dampened her enthusiasm one bit.

Ryan's story was the most romantic one she'd ever heard. Imagine—he'd flunked out as a teenager, and now, a mature man, he was determined to erase the black mark on his record. And he'd made the dean's list, which was not easy at Rosemont.

Jill was fascinated by his dedication, and she felt more in love with him than ever!

Now if only she could make him look up from the books, even just once, to notice that she was a real live girl who wanted to share some of his life.

ELEVEN

"Toni? I'm so glad you're home!" Jill said into the telephone receiver. "I called earlier, but you were out."

"Jill, hi." Toni sounded really happy to hear her friend. "I'm glad you caught me. I'm not home too much—ever. If I'm not out with Brandt at the theater, I visit my parents. Dad's doing really well, by the way."

"Then it's a miracle that I reached you," Jill said. "But listen, Toni, I need advice. And I started to write you another letter, but I knew you wouldn't write back."

"What do you mean? I write! How you can insult me like this, Jill, I'll never understand, when you're supposed to be my very best friend."

"Toni, you know and I know that you hate to write letters. So please don't be offended."

Toni made a loud sniffing sound. "Well, all right, I'll try to overlook the insult this time."

"Toni, cut it out! I'm standing here with my vast collection of quarters, but they won't last forever."

Out of Love

"Okay. So what's the problem, Jill? Tell Auntie Toni, and I'll try to give you the benefit of my years of wisdom."

Jill smiled. She could just picture Toni at the other end of the line, waving her hands around dramatically to emphasize her sweeping statements. Jill felt a sharp pang of homesickness.

"I'm calling about Ryan. You know, the older man I wrote to you about?"

"Oh, right. The dream guy with the beard. Have you kissed him yet, Jill? I've always wanted to kiss a guy with a beard."

"So have I, Toni, but no. This guy is really a problem."

"He already has a girlfriend, hmmm?" Toni sounded sympathetic.

"No, I don't think so. I think that my only rival is—schoolwork. He's driven by ambition, determined to make the dean's list every semester, and he pours absolutely all his energy into work."

Toni made a clucking sound. "In that case, he sounds suspiciously like a nerd, Jill. Maybe you'd better cross him off your list and move on to the next guy."

"Toni! Will you stop! Listen to me. Ryan is not a nerd. He's handsome and intelligent, and funny and caring, and he's so *alone* that it makes my heart break."

"What do you mean, alone?"

"I mean, living all alone in a crummy half-furnished apartment, with no food and no companionship, and nobody to tidy up his place for him—"

"Uh, oh. You want to mother him, don't you? I can tell." Toni's voice was laced with disapproval.

Jill hesitated before answering. "Yes, in a way. But mostly I want to be his girlfriend, Toni, if that's possible. The trouble is, he thinks I'm a kid. He's twenty-two—you see—and I look like a baby to him."

"Hmmm. I see what you mean. That is a problem. Of course with *me* it was no trouble at all because I always seem so much more mature than eighteen, so naturally Brandt just assumed—"

"Toni! Don't start making up stories, please."

"Okay, okay. So I'm this short little shrimp who probably looks more like twelve than eighteen. But you, Jill, you're tall and regal and pretty. You should have no problem coming across as older."

"Thanks for the compliment, but nothing is working with Ryan. You wouldn't believe all the chances I've had, too. I even went to his apartment!"

"You did? I'm scandalized, Jill."

"Oh, give me a break. Do you know how long I was there? About fifteen minutes—long enough to make and gulp a cup of coffee and hear part of the story of his life."

"Hmmm. Doesn't sound too romantic to me."

"It *wasn't*! That's what I'm trying to tell you. There is absolutely no romance in this man, at least none that I can see. So I want to know what I can do to—to change his viewpoint."

Toni cleared her throat importantly. "You've come to the right place, Jill. Even though you made me swear that I'd never interfere in your life again, I'm going to break that solemn vow and give you some advice. Because, tell me, have I ever steered you wrong?"

"Yes," Jill said.

"I'll ignore that. Jill, what you are going to do is this: you are going to learn to look and dress older."

"I am?"

"Absolutely. And we are talking not only clothes, Jill, but a new, mature hairstyle, and makeup, and high heels. We are talking a complete make-over, my friend. I only wish I could be there myself, to supervise it."

"Hmmm. You might have something there, Toni," Jill said, feeling suddenly excited. "But how will I bring about this major transformation?"

"There must be someone in that swanky school who can help you. Someone who knows fashion and can give you advice."

"I can't think of anyone offhand. I mean, there are a lot of preppy types, but they look like schoolgirls."

"No, no preppies. We want high fashion. The career girl look. A yuppie who's ready to plunge into the night life of Manhattan."

"That's a tall order, Toni." Jill felt discouraged.

"Don't worry, you'll find someone who can help. Just keep your eyes open. And when you have made your metamorphosis into this marvelous butterfly, I want you to take a photo—and send it to me, fast. Because I will have to know exactly how you look."

"Sure—okay. But listen, even if I do turn into this femme fatale, where will I wear these clothes? To psych class?"

"Oh, you'll think of someplace, Jill, never fear. You know, this is the eighties. These days a woman can invite a man out, and no one thinks any less of her. You could always invite him out to dinner."

"Sure. With what money?"

"These are only minor details," Toni said expansively. "First things first, and that means the 'new Jill.'"

The operator broke in just then. "Your three minutes are up," she said. "Please deposit more change."

"I'm running out of change," Jill said in a panic. "I have to hang up, Toni."

"Okay. Good luck. I miss you, Jill."

"Oh, I miss you too—terribly. So long for now."

"Bye."

Jill didn't have time to think about the "great transformation." She had another column to write and couldn't think of a topic.

"I thought you were going to write about the water polo club?" asked Terrence, walking with her from psychology class to the library.

"Oh, not yet. I haven't been in it long enough to have gathered any funny stories," Jill said. "I don't know. This is the first time that I've been stumped for a topic."

Terrence looked really worried for her. "Let me think. How about something humorous about freshman homesickness?"

"How can that be humorous?" Jill asked, but then she stopped to think about it. "Oh, wait a minute. I see. At first it seems as though you're going to *die* from the disease, and then, little by little, it fades away—sort of like the chicken pox—and pretty soon it's something that you can look back on and laugh about."

Terrence was looking at her with admiration. "There. You've practically got your column written, Jill. That metaphor about the chicken pox is perfect."

"Do you think so?" Jill stopped walking and looked up at Terrence. "Wow. I really have to thank you, Terrence. I don't know why you're giving me all these good story ideas when you could be using them yourself."

"As the comedian said, I've got a million of 'em." To show that he was joking, Terrence smiled broadly—and Jill felt a strange little catch in her throat. Why was there something so familiar about Terrence, especially when he smiled, something that made her want to stand back and take a long, good look? She felt as though she'd known him a long time and that there was some reason why she ought to be avoiding him—but for the life of her, she couldn't imagine why.

Stop being so prejudiced against him, she told herself. *You have absolutely no reason to feel this way.* And she didn't, she realized. She had kidded about Terrence being too young for her, but that wasn't it at all. In many ways, he was more mature than the average college freshman. He was certainly intelligent and hardworking—and he was a good, caring friend.

But who was it that he *reminded* her of?

Terrence was aware of her staring at him. "Is something wrong?" he asked lightly. "Do I have mustard on my shirt or something?"

"Oh, of course not! I keep—keep thinking that you look like someone else I know, but I can't figure out who. It's nothing."

"Jill? Can I ask you something?"

"Certainly." She was looking through her books to make sure she had her notebook.

His green eyes were sparkling in the morning sunshine. "Do you think you're ever going to be ready to have that cup of coffee with me?"

Terrence wasn't really talking about coffee, of course, and Jill knew it. He was saying, "Will I ever have a chance?"

She felt she had to answer carefully. "I think so, Terrence. I just need—I just need a little more time. I'm still getting used to not being Craig's girlfriend."

Terrence didn't argue with that. But Jill felt like a big liar, and she didn't like herself for it. The truth was, she wanted to set her sights on just one target: Ryan Davis.

Out of Love

Why can't things stay nice and simple, she thought. *Why can't Terrence be satisfied that he and I are good friends?*

TWELVE

Cassandra wandered into the room just as Jill was finishing her column for the week.

"Hi, ho," Cassandra said, slipping out of the medieval-style cape with a hood that she sometimes wore on chilly afternoons. "Haven't seen much of you lately, roommate."

"No. I guess I've been awfully busy." Jill put down her pen and turned in her desk chair. "Cassie, do you ever get homesick?"

Cassandra made a face. "Are you conducting research, or do you really want to know for yourself?"

"Well—a little of both," Jill admitted. "I did just write a column about freshman homesickness. But I don't really need any new material. I only wondered because—well, because I don't know all that much about you, Cassie."

"What is there to know?" Cassandra shrugged and tossed back her thick black hair in a careless gesture. "You know that half the dorm thinks I'm a witch—"

98

"No, they don't. Not really."

Cassandra smiled. "Okay. Let's say that I've behaved in a way to *make* half the dorm think I'm a witch. And they know I have a cat that acts as my familiar—" She looked down fondly at Jelly Bean, who was nestled against a pillow on her bed.

"Jelly Bean is adorable, Cassie, but she doesn't make you a witch—unless we get caught by the dean of students and then we'll say you need the cat because you're a witch." Jill still worried about breaking the strict no-pets rule of Rosemont College, but she felt Jelly Bean was worth the risk. Cassandra made a perfect roommate, and Cassandra and Jelly Bean came as a package.

"Jelly Bean is pretty cute, isn't she?" Cassandra said now.

Jill tried again. "Cassie, I know that you love animals. And I know that you traveled to India and are a vegetarian—but really, what else do I know about you? Almost nothing. I've never pried, have I?"

"Nope." Cassandra pulled a book out of her half of the bookcase. "That's what I've always liked about you, Jill."

"So you don't want to tell me whether you've ever been homesick?"

Cassandra looked Jill right in the eye. "If you had a home like mine you'd never get homesick, Jill. *Sick* of home, yes, but never homesick."

"Are your parents really that bad?"

"I've already told you. Mummy Dearest is absolutely always right about everything and always knows just how little Cassandra should be dressed and what boys she should date—"

"And your dad?"

"Oh, he's not so bad. He's a good doctor, I'll say that for him. I admire him for doing his best in the crazy world of medicine. But why do we have to rake all this up now, Jill?"

"I don't know. I've been thinking that we haven't been much in the way of close friends, Cassie. What do you think? Want to do something together tonight?"

Cassandra looked at Jill with suspicion. "Like what? You know I usually take a walk at night and sometimes I write a poem as I walk—"

"Well, how about breaking tradition for once? Instead of going out alone, let me go walking with you."

"But you always go to the cafeteria for your supper, Jill, and I don't like the food there."

"I know. You hate to watch us eat the flesh of murdered animals." Jill shuddered at the very words. "So how about this? Instead of your eating a container of yogurt all alone tonight, what if we both treat ourselves to a meal in town? There's a health food restaurant where you can get a great vegetarian salad."

Cassie still looked suspicious. "I don't get it, Jill. Up to now we've been roommates who never bothered each other, and that was the beauty of it all."

"I only thought—" Jill felt a stab of hurt. "Oh, never mind. I suppose it was a silly idea." She turned back to her desk and looked over the column she'd just written.

There was silence for a few minutes. Cassandra went out the door and immediately came bursting back in, as though she'd just that minute arrived.

"Why, Jill, *hi*!" she said in a pleasant, not too exaggerated way. "What a nice surprise, finding you in. What do you say we have supper together tonight?"

Jill looked at her with eyes that were sparkling with tears.

"Come on, Jill, what are friends for, anyway?" Cassandra said, looking as though she were enjoying this new role. "I'd like to treat you to dinner in town. Get your coat on, girl."

"What made you change your mind?" Jill managed to ask.

Cassandra smiled. "You. You sitting there looking sort of down in the dumps and homesick. I can't understand homesickness, but I can respect the fact that plenty of kids do get it."

"Like the chicken pox," Jill said, nodding. "That's what I compared homesickness to, in my column—the chicken pox. And you know what? The more I wrote about it, the more I realized that I was thinking of home. Mom's cooking. Dad reading the newspaper. My cat at home, purring for some

Little Friskies. Toni bursting in at any old time of day or night with one of her crazy schemes—"

"Yep, you've got it bad, all right," Cassandra pronounced. "I can tell, I'm a doctor's daughter, after all. And the only remedy is a dinner away from this campus."

"With a friend?" Jill added.

"Absolutely! Of course, with a friend. What do you think I am, just this weird person who doesn't know how to be a decent roommate—and friend?"

Jill wiped away the few little tears that had gathered in her eyes.

"Let's go, get a move on," Cassandra urged. "I'm getting hungry!"

"So that's what I've been doing lately," Jill finished saying in answer to Cassandra's inquiry. The two girls were sitting at a booth, munching their salads, in Daisy's Health Food Café.

"Sounds pretty active. Water polo, your column, your new friend Terrence—" And here Cassandra smiled, making her whole face look really pretty under her long mane of dark hair. "And chasing after someone named Ryan. Well, well. I never dreamed you were leading this exciting secret life, Jill."

"Exciting, sure," Jill said and stabbed her fork into a mound of bean sprouts. "Isn't there any protein in this salad?"

"Of course. The kidney beans and the tofu. There's nothing like tofu."

"I'm afraid to ask what it is. Some kind of soybean thing, isn't it?"

"Soybean curd. Delicious and nutritious. And nobody had to kill a living animal to get it."

"Yes, well, actually it isn't too awful," Jill admitted. "But this doesn't mean that I intend to become a vegetarian, Cassie."

"Of course not. Did I ever ask you to?"

Jill smiled. "So now I've told you enough about me. What have you been doing, besides writing poetry?"

Cassandra looked down at her salad as though there were something very important there. "Not an awful lot, Jill. I try to keep up with schoolwork, but as you know, it doesn't interest me very much."

"I know. You'd rather be traveling across India than be here at Rosemont."

"Right. Well, I keep my hand in with all the animal societies. The A.S.P.C.A.—Save the Whales organization. The Society for Baby Seal Preservation—"

"No boyfriend, Cassie? Not even at home?"

"Oh, there's that boy in physics class, but he's just a friend—for now." Cassandra looked Jill straight in the eye. "I'm not as comfortable with guys as you are, Jill."

"Me? I don't seem to be doing such a great job of attracting anyone. At least not the one I want."

Cassie toyed with her salad. "But you try, and that's what counts, isn't it? I really have to admit that I admire you sometimes, Jill."

"That's crazy. I'm always admiring *you*, for being so independent."

"Did you ever think that a person might be independent because she's basically shy?"

Jill was amazed. "I'd never think of you as shy, Cassie. Why, you're—you're so confident and so active in things that are adult—"

Cassie smiled. "Still, it is a possibility that a person who doesn't relate well to kids her own age could be shy—and could be hoping to fall madly in love with some man, the way you have—"

Cassie changed the subject abruptly. "Speaking of men, take a look, Jill. Who's that bearded guy at the door who's staring at you?"

Jill turned toward the door, feeling the familiar thumping of her heart. *It's him!*

"That's Ryan Davis," Jill whispered. "The Ryan I've been telling you about." She couldn't believe it when he walked over to their table as soon as she had spotted him.

"Hello, ladies," he said cheerfully.

"Hello, Ryan," Jill greeted. "What are you doing here? Are you a vegetarian, too, like my roommate?"

"Not exactly."

"Oh," Jill said, remembering her manners. "Ryan, this is my roommate, Cassandra. Cassie, this is Ryan Davis. The T.A. from my psych class."

"Nice to meet you," Ryan and Cassie said at the same time.

Jill could see that Cassie was looking Ryan over, finding him quite interesting. And then Jill felt her roommate give her a slight kick under the table.

Just like something Toni would do, Jill thought with a flush of happiness. It was a friend's way of saying, "Hmmm, he's definitely okay, and I'll do all I can to help—"

"Is this where you eat your meals, Ryan?" Jill asked.

He laughed. "Not all the time. I come in when I'm really busy with studying, just to grab a cheese sandwich. I think it's goat cheese, but I don't dare ask."

"On whole grain bread, I hope?" Cassie asked.

"Oh, of course. And with alfalfa sprouts. Nothing like those sprouts to increase the brain matter." Ryan's eyes were twinkling with amusement.

"You can join us if you'd like," Cassie said, and Jill almost fell off her chair. That was totally unlike Cassandra, who usually kept her distance from new people.

"Well, why not?" Ryan said and pulled up a chair. "I eat alone most of the time. It'll be nice to have someone to talk to for a change."

The waitress took his order for a bowl of lentil soup and tofu lasagna.

Cassandra was staring at him. "So you *are* a vegetarian!" she said enthusiastically.

"Sorry, no." Ryan settled back comfortably in his chair. "I enjoy the food here at Daisy's, but

105

there's nothing I like better than a good steak or plate of spaghetti and meatballs."

"Oh, me, too," Jill said fervently. "In fact, I was just thinking of my mother's meatballs this evening—"

"And becoming terminally homesick, I might add," Cassandra said with a grin. "That's why we're here," she told Ryan. "Because we had to chase away Jill's homesick blues."

"Oh, no, that was just a momentary thing," Jill lied. She didn't want Ryan to think she was always blubbering about something.

"Hey, don't deny your feelings," Ryan said. "Bring them out in the open. That's the only way we learn to cope, you know."

"You have *got* to be a psych major," Cassandra said dryly, and the three of them laughed.

They chatted easily throughout the rest of the dinner, and Jill continued to be amazed at Cassandra's friendliness. In fact, for a few shaky moments she began to wonder if Cassie were getting too interested in Ryan—for herself.

But Cassie dispelled her doubts. "If you two are so eager for a spaghetti and meatball dinner— ugh!—" she made a face—"it so happens that I have two tickets to a spaghetti supper that I do not intend to ever use." She fumbled in her shoulder bag and came up with the tickets.

"What the—" Jill asked. "Why do you have these?"

"I bought them, silly. You see—they're for a benefit for the animal shelter here in town. As soon as I heard about the cause, I knew I had to make a contribution."

"Even though you knew you wouldn't go to the dinner?"

Cassandra shrugged. "I was going to throw the tickets away. But maybe you guys can use them. It sounds as though it's one of those all-you-can-eat things at a lodge here in town."

Ryan was looking at the tickets and then at Cassandra, as though he couldn't quite believe it.

"Can you afford to throw money away like that?" he asked bluntly.

"I'm not throwing it away, I donated it to something I believe in. A bigger shelter for stray dogs and cats."

"Cassandra is an incurable animal lover," Jill explained. "She'd do anything for a worthy cause— even swim to Newfoundland to club the people who club the baby seals, I think."

"Of course I would," Cassandra said gravely.

"Well, this dinner sounds great. I for one would love to go to it, if you really mean it, Cassie," Ryan said. "What about you, Jill? Do you want to check it out? The meatballs might not be as good as your mother's, but how can you argue with all-you-can-eat?"

Jill stammered for a moment. "I—I can't argue with it," she said. "When is this dinner?"

"Saturday night, it says here." Ryan was staring at her expectantly. "If you're game, I'll pick you up and we can go together. What do you say?"

"Well—" Jill felt another kick from Cassandra under the table. "Well, sure. Sure I'll go."

It would be almost like a date, she thought giddily. Ryan would be picking her up at the dorm, and she would be—she hoped—the New Jill, by then. Just as Toni had predicted, she would have her chance to be all dressed up and looking impressively mature.

Ryan would find himself out with a woman of the world.

Thank you, Cassie, she thought gratefully. *You really have turned out to be a true friend.*

THIRTEEN

"This is going to be a major challenge—but I think we can pull it off," said Marcie. She and her roommate, Heather, were standing over Jill, who'd been plunked down into a chair in the older girls' room.

"What's going on here?" Cassandra asked, peering into the room at just that moment.

"High-level strategy conference," Marcie told her. "Can we—or can we not—turn this girl into a high-fashion beauty in just a couple of days?"

"Why would she want you to?" Cassandra looked at Jill as though she had suddenly turned purple. "Jill, is this for real? You want these girls to change the way you look?"

Jill squirmed with embarrassment. "I asked them if they could help, Cassie. You see, I want to look older—if I can—for my date on Saturday with Ryan."

"That's crazy," Cassie groaned. "In the first place, going to that meatball dinner is not really a date, do you think? And in the second place, why don't you want to go as yourself? What's wrong with Jill Gardner?"

"She wants to look mature, Cassie," Heather said impatiently. "Because this guy is so much older—"

"But he likes Jill just the way she is. I can tell." Cassandra gave one of her noncommittal shrugs. "But, hey, to each her own. I just hope you don't ruin her!"

"Don't you worry about a thing," Marcie told Jill in a soothing voice after Cassandra had wandered away. "We know a lot about this sort of thing. Heather's mother is a dress designer, and I worked in a beauty salon once, two summers ago—"

"As a beautician?"

"Well, no, I was the receptionist. But I did learn an awful lot of stuff about beauty. You're in good hands, Jill."

The two worked on Jill's face for hours, experimenting with various colors of makeup. After they'd designed just the face they liked, they went to work on her hair. The upsweep, they finally agreed, was the most sophisticated style for Jill and her particular length of reddish-brown hair.

"And we'll do it for you just like this on Saturday," they promised as Jill studied her "new look" in Heather's full-length mirror.

"Yeah, we'll even pin some exotic flowers in each curl."

"But my hair's not curly," Jill said.

110

"It will be, don't worry. And as for clothes—just leave those to us."

"She's an easy size to fit," Heather said, staring at Jill's slim build. "No problem in borrowing clothes."

"Oh, I don't know about borrowing clothes. I've never—"

"Relax, Jill, will you? This is such an exciting challenge that every girl in the dorm is going to be interested. Fascinated, even. You'll see. They'll all want to donate their absolute best things."

Jill sighed, but deep down she did feel relieved. She was certain that if she could look truly, awesomely beautiful, just once, Ryan would notice that she was more than an immature little freshman.

Dear Toni,

Just a quick note to tell you that I'm following your advice. These two seniors across the hall, Heather and Marcie, know *everything* about fashion, and they've been experimenting with me for a couple of days now.

And the results are fantastic! They've got all the girls in the dorm in on this—and plenty of the boys, too. They've come up with clothes that you wouldn't believe! Expensive stuff, Toni, and so elegant. They all want me to borrow something of theirs!

Heather did take a photo, and I'll be sending it to you when we get the film developed. In the meantime, just picture me: hair piled high, flowers set into each carefully made curl, and my face made up good enough for any model.

The dress they've chosen for me is blue silk, a straight, sleek one with padded shoulders and a scooped V-back. It goes perfectly with my blue heels—the really high ones I bought for the prom.

I'm wearing sexy stockings with designs on them and jewelry from the richest girls at Rosemont.

And perfume! They all came charging at me with their favorite brands, and I had to try each one until I began to smell like a soap factory! We finally decided on Allure, because that's how they said I look—alluring!

I keep looking in the mirror and thinking, *Is this me*? Jill Gardner, the quiet one who writes the column and studies all the time? Or even the water polo player who looks like a drowned rat at the end of practice?

Oh, and most important of all, Ryan and I have a date. Sort of. Not exactly a real date, I suppose, but it's too good a chance to pass up. We're going to a meatball dinner at some lodge in town. Don't laugh, Toni. I know that doesn't sound very romantic, but it's the best I could manage, for now.

Well, it's almost time for him to arrive. I'll

let you know what happens—are your fingers crossed for me?

Love, Jill

The entire dorm turned out, trying to look inconspicuous, when Jill was finally and totally ready for her date with Ryan at five-thirty. Kids were lined up on the stairway and overflowing the lounge area, as well as perched and cold on the front porch.

"I wish everybody wasn't hanging around like this," Jill complained to Marcie.

"Nothing we can do about it, hon. They're all curious to see this magnificent man—and his reaction to the new you!"

"Just relax, Jill," Heather told her. "We'll be discreet. We only want to observe."

Jill felt more and more nervous as the time drew near for Ryan to arrive. She paced around her room in her prom shoes, wobbling a little because she wasn't used to wearing such high heels. She stared at the array of coats on her bed—all donations from the girls in the dorm. She had finally decided on Marcie's elegant beige coat because it was the most sophisticated of all.

"Here he comes, Jill," someone called out who was watching the path to McGregor.

"If he has a beard, that's him," Marcie said. "Oh, Lord. You look like a vision, Jill—an absolute vision. We've added so many years to you that you could probably apply for Social Security, right now."

"Gee, thanks," Jill said, smiling.

"You know what I mean. You look grown-up, kid, and svelte, and rich, and—oh, I can't believe we did such a great job! Can you, Heather?"

"Nope," Heather said, chomping on her gum excitedly.

Cassandra had been sitting quietly through all this, trying to read one of the Russian novels in her vast collection of books. "I hope you know what you're doing, Jill," she said in a flat voice.

"I hope so, too, Cassie." Jill was beginning to feel frightened. But she knew she had to go through with it.

Ryan entered McGregor with a deep frown creasing his forehead. "What are all the people doing here tonight?" he asked one of the students. "I never saw such a crowd—is it a dorm meeting or something?"

"Naw, just a slow night, I guess," said the student, a boy named Charles from the third floor.

Jill's friend Robert said, "Everybody seems to feel like hanging out, that's all."

Ryan shook his head in bewilderment. And just then Jill walked out of her room, making the grand entrance that she had been practicing for hours.

Someone began to whistle the tune, "There she is—Miss America—" and Jill gasped in horror. How could anyone embarrass her like that? She stumbled on her high-heeled shoes and fell right into Ryan's arms.

Ryan began to chuckle. "Whoa, there, Jill. Are you okay?" he asked as he helped Jill gain her balance.

"I'm fine," Jill said with as much dignity as she could summon. "And I'm ready to leave, right now."

"Er—are you really going to wear those shoes? I don't have a car, you know. We have to walk the whole way into town." Ryan sounded apologetic.

"Why, certainly. I can manage," Jill said bravely, going out the front door. "No problem. I used to wear high heels all the time, back home."

"Good night now, Jill," a group of the boys called out in singsong fashion on the front porch. "Be sure and have a good time," they chorused as one.

"I could kill them," she muttered as she and Ryan walked off. "I mean, haven't they ever seen anyone going out to dinner before?"

Ryan's grin lit up his whole face. "I must admit, I've never seen a turnout like that in my whole life. Why are they so curious, anyway?"

"Who knows?" Jill sputtered. "They're just terribly immature."

"Oh, I don't know." Ryan put out a hand to steady Jill, who was not doing too well on her heels. "They're probably a lot of fun at dorm parties. Are you absolutely sure, Jill, that you want to wear those stilts?"

"Certainly," she said.

"Well—" Ryan looked doubtful but they kept walking.

The walk to town was pure torture for Jill, although she tried not to let it show. She teetered and she tottered, but she kept a carefully controlled face and tried to talk intelligently about things that she thought Ryan would be interested in.

"Ryan, how long have you known that you wanted to be a psychologist?"

"For several years now. Whoops, watch out. If you step into a pothole you'll break your neck—" He grabbed her again and kept her from falling over.

Jill struggled to remain unruffled. "Well, it certainly must be interesting. I mean, studying the behavior of human beings."

"And all their funny little foibles," Ryan said almost under his breath.

"Yes," Jill said, not realizing what she'd agreed to. "I must say that I plan to take more psychology courses. Professor Blake is such an inspiring teacher that he—yikes!" She almost fell headfirst into a large forsythia bush.

"Maybe we ought to get a cab, Jill."

"No, no, I think we're almost there," she argued. And, in fact, they weren't too far from the lodge. Jill's biggest disappointment, so far, had been Ryan's not commenting on her "great transformation." *Well, maybe he just thinks this is the real me, the one he hadn't noticed until now,* she thought. In that case, all Marcie and Heather's work had been well worthwhile.

The lodge was rather a shabby place, but the delicious aroma of the spaghetti sauce was suddenly wafting all around them as they went inside. Ryan presented their tickets, and they waited in a long line to be seated.

"Good turnout," he commented, looking around. "I guess the people of this town really care about animals."

"Or about spaghetti dinners," Jill said, smiling. She felt better now that she was standing still in line, and not coping with her heels.

They were seated at last, but it wasn't exactly romantic. Two families with children were on either side of them, and a swarm of kids dominated the table.

"Yeccch! The meatballs are *gross*," shouted a pair of twins who were beside Jill. "We're not going to eat these, Ma!"

"Of course you are, Jeremy. And, Jordan, stop twirling your spaghetti like that! You'll drop it into the nice lady's lap."

Terrified, Jill backed away from the boisterous twins. She could just imagine how she'd feel if she went back to the dorm with the borrowed dress all stained with spaghetti sauce.

The noise became louder and louder as the hall filled up. Ryan didn't seem terribly bothered by the racket, but Jill found that her appetite had left her. Was it for this—this circus—that she had gotten so dressed up?

"Mmm, the spaghetti's great," Ryan told her. "Eat up, Jill. Might as well get our money's worth. Or should I say, Cassie's money's worth?"

The twins were now playing splash games with their glasses of grape soda. "Somehow I don't seem to be hungry," Jill said, backing farther away from the obstreperous children.

"That's too bad." Ryan was eating as though he hadn't had a hot meal in months. "This is excellent."

Even the cafeteria at Rosemont was better than *this*, Jill thought in dismay.

Jill passed on dessert, too, which was a bowlful of ice cream. Jeremy and Jordan, however, opted for chocolate, and the gobs of ice cream poised on their spoons became dangerous weapons as Jill continued to worry about the beautiful blue silk dress.

Finally Ryan looked at her sympathetically. "Guess you're ready to leave this place, hmm, Jill? These kids are kind of a pain—"

"Yes, they are, sort of."

"Well, you sure were a good sport about it." Ryan smiled at her and patted her hand briefly. His touch made her feel a hundred times better. It also set her dreaming of a kiss—

They stood up, ready to leave, and the twins yelled "goodbye" to them.

What happens now? she wondered. *Does he take me right back to my dorm, and that's the end of the date?*

"Since you're so dressed up," Ryan said, "it would be a shame to end the evening already. Do you feel like seeing a movie, Jill?"

Her heart began to beat fast.

"Yes, that sounds great," she said. A date! A real date at last! And how wonderful that she was looking her absolute best, thanks to Heather and Marcie.

FOURTEEN

This will be my big chance to show how sophisticated I am, Jill thought as they crossed the room to the exit. They went outside, walked across the parking lot—and then the rain started in one huge deluge. Sheets of it washed over them.

"Oh, no," Jill whispered in horror. "Not rain—"

"Don't be upset," Ryan said. "I can call a cab for us."

"It's too late already," Jill said under her breath. She could feel the makeup running down her face, and she fumbled in her purse for a wad of tissues. At least she could try to save Marcie's coat from the makeup.

"What do you mean, too late?" Ryan was standing there watching her as she mopped away at her face. "Oh. Your face has all these streaks of brown and blue on it," he said, fascinated. "What's going on?"

"What's coming off is more like it," Jill said morosely.

"I didn't know you were wearing so much makeup," Ryan said thoughtfully.

120

"You mean you didn't even notice?" she asked.

The rain continued to pelt down on them, and Jill's hairdo came tumbling down, as well.

"What's the *use*?" she said out loud. "I try to look like somebody glamorous, and this is what I get—a spaghetti dinner with the Dennis the Menace twins and now—a flood."

"Jill," Ryan spoke in a low voice, "come on over here, under this tree. It'll give us a little shelter."

"But it's already too late, the damage is done. Can't you see? I look like Bozo the Clown!"

Gently, Ryan dabbed at Jill's face with a clean handkerchief that he had in his pocket. "I can't imagine why you wanted to wear all this makeup," he said. "This stuff isn't you at all. You're so pretty the way you look naturally, Jill. Don't you realize that?"

She let out a big sob that had been bursting to erupt. "Thank you, Ryan, but—I just wanted to look *older*, that's all. And obviously I've failed—miserably."

Ryan kept his hand on her cheek for a second. "Why did you want to look older? You're eighteen, aren't you? What's wrong with that? That's a wonderful age to be."

"I'm a baby—compared to you, Ryan. I just wanted—I just wanted—" And that's when her hair tumbled down completely, scattering flowers all over her shoulders.

Ryan spoke in a soft, calm voice. "I'm beginning to see what you wanted. You thought—oh, Jill,

I never wanted you to be older. I think you're perfect the way you are. You're a really sweet kid."

At that she burst into full-blown tears, even though she knew that crying would make her look more babyish. And the crying had a surprising effect: Ryan folded her into his arms comfortingly. She burrowed her face into his jacket and inhaled his masculine scent. He was so strong, so controlled, and so much—older.

"It seems as though you're always consoling me," Jill said between gulps and sobs.

"That's okay," Ryan answered softly, his lips against her cheek. "It's not every day I get to hold a pretty girl in my arms."

Startled, she looked up at him. Was this it? Was this the beginning of romance? But he didn't kiss her.

"Besides, it's hard being a freshman. I remember so well," Ryan added, giving her a pat like a father or a fond uncle.

Jill's heart plummeted. She had really believed, just for a moment, that Ryan was about to make a declaration. But instead they pulled apart, and Jill had to dry her eyes.

"Okay," she said, sounding more in control. "You're right. All this makeup was silly. The girls in the dorm wanted to make Jill look glamorous."

Ryan laughed. "They succeeded, in a way. But maybe you'll feel better if we go see a movie. Do you still want to go?"

She smiled as though nothing at all were wrong.

"Sure," she said with enthusiasm.

The only theater in town was featuring a Humphrey Bogart film festival, which didn't thrill Jill very much but seemed to interest Ryan a lot.

"I love Bogart! Have you ever seen *Casablanca*?" he asked.

"No." She didn't add that she'd always thought of Bogart as a too-macho tough guy. The old films that Jill liked were the really romantic ones.

But she was pleasantly surprised by *Key Largo* and *Casablanca*. Humphrey Bogart could be romantic after all, she realized.

There didn't seem to be any spark of romance in Ryan Davis, however, she thought bleakly. He didn't so much as put an arm around her during the two films. He didn't even attempt to hold her hand. He just sat there enjoying the pictures, munching on popcorn, and acting as though he hadn't been to a movie in a very long time.

It was frustrating, to say the least. Jill had never had trouble attracting boys. She'd had plenty of dates back in high school and several steady boyfriends, including Eric, long before, and, of course, Craig. There had even been Carlo, in Venice, Italy, who loved her enough to want to marry her and keep her in Europe.

But Ryan was a real puzzle.

He did call a taxi for the trip back to campus because the rain hadn't let up at all.

"Well, those films were really good," Jill admitted as they drove to the campus.

"You really liked them?" Ryan looked pleased.

"I really did. I can see that Bogie was a very sensitive actor, and I'm glad I had a chance to realize that."

"He was a complex man," Ryan said thoughtfully.

"Spoken like a true psych major," she said teasingly.

Ryan screwed up his face in a Bogie imitation. "Humphrey was an all right guy, shweetheart," he quipped out of the side of his mouth.

And Jill's knees turned to absolute mush. If only she could believe that Ryan would really call *her* sweetheart someday, she'd be the happiest girl on earth!

The cab stopped in front of McGregor Hall.

"Please tell Cassie how much I enjoyed the dinner," Ryan said, running around and opening the taxi door for Jill. "Especially the meatballs, make sure to add that."

"Oh, no. As a vegetarian, she'd be grossed out!"

"I know." He grinned like a mischievous kid and walked Jill to the door.

"You like to tease, don't you?" Jill said, hobbling along the path in her destroyed shoes.

"Sure. I have two younger sisters," Ryan explained. "I've learned to be a master at the art of teasing."

They had reached the porch of the dorm, and Jill could tell that he wasn't going to kiss her. No way. Not the way she looked, with her hair falling around her shoulders like the spaghetti at dinner, and the makeup streaks still smudging her face.

But she tried to look on the bright side. They'd had a date, anyway, and maybe Ryan would begin to think of her as someone who was fun to date. Maybe he'd come around after all, in time.

"Thanks for a nice time tonight," she said politely.

"Oh. Thank you, too. It was fun."

They stood there looking at each other for a quiet moment.

"For what it's worth," he said in a quiet voice, "I think you're a very mature eighteen-year-old."

"Oh." She was dumbfounded.

Ryan whistled a tune as he returned to the waiting taxi.

Dear Toni,

I think I may give up for a while. After my "date" with Ryan, I honestly believe that it doesn't matter to him whether I'm eighteen or twenty-two. Or even forty-two!

Here's the photo, so you can see how I looked before the rains came. When the rain got done with my makeup, I looked like a Jackson Pollock painting. You know, those paintings that are all dribbles and spatters of paint.

But I really was a knockout, for a while. Ryan didn't respond to the New Jill in the least, except to tell me that I was prettier without makeup! So I think I'm going to stop chasing him for now. If he wants to see me again, it'll have to be up to him.

I know, I can just hear you saying, "You should never give up, Jill." But there comes a moment in every relationship when a girl has to stop and take a good look. I'm doing that. And what I see is a man who evidently likes living alone, likes working hard to make the dean's list, and who doesn't mind his lonely life-style.

Anyway, I thank you for your words of wisdom. It was good advice, Auntie Toni, and it probably would have worked on any *other* older male. But Ryan Davis is just impossible.

I hope all is well with you, Toni. I'd like to beg you to write a letter, but I suppose you'd get all insulted. So instead I'll say that I *expect* a letter from you any day now.

Other than Ryan, things are going good here. My schoolwork had been very hard, as I knew it would be, but I manage to keep up and even pull a few A's along with the B's. I can't complain about that!

Cassandra and I have been getting more chummy ever since I talked her into going to Daisy's with me. That's a health food café where you're not allowed to even mention the word "meat" for fear of someone chasing after you with a vegetable chopper.

I've been to a couple of water polo practices now, and I'm not doing too badly. It takes awhile to learn how to "dribble" and do lob shots and all the other maneuvers in the water, but I'm working on it. Since the club is just for fun, it seems as though the captain might let me play in the upcoming game against Morris College. I'm really looking forward to that!

Take care, and remember I'm *expecting* a letter from you. This very week.

Lots of love, Jill

FIFTEEN

"I'm really psyched," Jill said to Suzie late Monday afternoon. "This'll be my first intermural competition in a long time."

"You didn't swim in high school?" Suzie asked with disbelief. The two girls were standing in front of the student union with the other members of the water polo team, waiting for their chartered bus to arrive.

"No. Only the swimming you do in gym, of course. But I kept up with my Red Cross lessons all these years."

"That's interesting," Suzie said. "So what made you decide to play water polo, of all things? I mean, it's such a rough game!"

"Guess I just needed to break a few of my old patterns," Jill said with a smile. "I was getting into a rut."

"Well, good for you," Suzie said. "Now who is *this* walking toward us? He's awful cute, but he's not on the team as far as I know."

"Why, that's Terrence," Jill said in surprise. "I wonder what he's—oh, I remember. He's going to cover the game for the *Voice*."

"Wow. We'll be getting some publicity. I must say, he *is* cute! Will you introduce me to him?" Suzie looked determined not to miss this opportunity. "Or—is he somebody special to you, Jill?" she added as an afterthought.

"Terrence? No. He's just a friend." Jill watched as the tall, easygoing freshman came striding toward her. Again, because of the cheerful way he smiled, and the way the light glinted in his green eyes, she had an unsettling sense of déjà vu—the feeling that she had known Terrence somewhere before, before Rosemont College. But she just couldn't put her finger on *where*.

"Hi, Jill," Terrence said. "I'll be taking the bus with your team. I actually was able to get Malcolm to allow it."

"Great," Jill said. "Listen, I'd like you to meet somebody, Terrence." And she proceeded to introduce Suzie to him. The petite, pretty blond made an immediate and obvious play for Terrence.

"My, you are tall," Suzie said, looking up at him as though he were Superman. "And you work on the school newspaper? You must be awfully smart. Me, I can never manage to put two sentences together in a creative way."

"Oh? I hope you're not an English major, then," Terrence said, looking amused.

"I most certainly am not," Suzie said. "I'm really into sports, so I might major in physical education. You know, be a P.E. teacher someday."

Suzie monopolized Terrence until the bus came rolling up to the curb. Then they all had to listen to Malcolm and his endless instructions.

"We're going to be a mature group of athletes today, on this bus and at Morris College. There will be no crazy stunts, I hope you all realize that! I'm quite serious about this, now."

"We know you are, Mal," Suzie said, pinching his cheeks. "And, oooh, you look so adorable when you're mad."

Malcolm glared at her. Behind the thick glasses, his eyes bulged with indignation. He looked as though girls should not pinch his cheeks!

In all the confusion, Suzie got separated from Terrence, and Jill found that when she took a seat on the bus, Terrence was right beside her. She was surprised. She thought he had been flattered by Suzie's flirting.

"I heard the club is having a party after the game," Terrence said. "Win or lose, they always celebrate with a pizza pig-out."

"Oh. Right. I did hear something about it," Jill said. Actually she had forgotten about it, she'd been so busy chasing Ryan. "Are you going to the party?" she asked Terrence.

"Sure, if you invite me." He settled back in his seat, smiling mischievously. "I'm not a member of the club, you see."

Jill felt uncomfortable. She had never been that close to Terrence before, and she noticed that he smelled absolutely wonderful, like a blend of after-shave and soap. It was unnerving.

"If I invite you?" she repeated absently. "Well, if that's all you need to go to the party, then, of course I'll invite you. Look at all the things you're always doing for me! Reminding me when I have psychology experiments and helping me with topics for my column—"

"You make me sound like a boy scout," Terrence said dryly. "Am I really that clean in thought, word, and deed?"

"As far as I know," Jill said, smiling with him. "I've never known you to be anything but clean."

You even smell clean, she thought again, and tried to banish the thought. It was wrong, some-how, feeling even the slightest bit attracted to Terrence. He wasn't the man she wanted—not at all!

"So. Have you been hanging around the *Voice* office much?" Jill asked, trying to think of a nice safe topic.

"Yes, now and then. Russel really is nice, and I've been learning a lot from him. And once in a while I see Jake Randall sitting there, batting out his deathless prose."

"He sure is a terrific writer," Jill said. "Did you read that piece in last week's issue about the football team? It was amazing."

"Yeah. Funny and yet right to the point, too." Terrence was staring right at Jill, making her feel like squirming. "Well, Jill, are you feeling ready to play in a real water polo game?"

"No. And yes," she said. "I'm scared, but I'm anxious to see if I have any talent for this game at all." She didn't add that she had the beginnings of a chest cold and felt less than energetic.

Just then Suzie managed to deposit herself in the seat right in front of Terrence. "Well, hi, there. I thought I'd lost you." She really was a shameless flirt, but Jill thought it was funny.

And she wondered how she'd feel if Terrence suddenly took a real interest in Suzie.

The question stayed in her mind throughout the water polo game against Morris College. Suppose she did see Terrence falling in love with Suzie—or any other girl, for that matter. Would she be upset? She told herself that she certainly shouldn't be. She didn't want him for herself, after all.

The game was exciting. Morris College had a good-sized pool and bleachers filled with at least fifty or sixty spectators. Since the entire room was walled with ceramic tile, it was like a giant echo chamber. The noise level, both from the players and the audience, was extremely high.

The game moved so fast that Jill, standing on the sidelines, could hardly follow it. One minute she saw the ball in one place, and seconds later it was zinging to the other side of the pool.

"Beat Rosemont, you guys," was the shout of the day from the Morris players, who were spirited and competitive. They were good players, though the roughness of the game really astounded Jill. The junior-high swim team had never been like this!

"Hey, Morris—kill Rosemont!" she heard people in the bleachers yelling. "Come on, McDuffy! Get them, Flanagan!"

The splashing was fierce, too. More than once Jill laughed when she saw Terrence and Malcolm, both in their clothes, getting doused by the chlorinated water.

"Suzie is a good player, isn't she?" Terrence remarked to Jill at one point.

"Yes," Jill replied in a clipped voice. "She looks good in her suit, too, doesn't she?" Terrence looked at her with amusement.

Jill got to play for only about three minutes of the twenty-eight-minute game, but that was enough to convince her that she wasn't yet in good enough shape for the superdemanding sport. She was aware, too, that besides the chest cold she was developing, she was getting a sore throat. She realized, too late, that she shouldn't have played at all.

"I'm going to have to get in a lot more swimming practice," she said to Suzie as the two of them stood by the side of the pool watching the last few minutes of action.

"Yeah, you really have to," Suzie told her. "Most of us manage to get to the pool every day, even if we just do laps of the butterfly and lots of eggbeater kicks."

"All of it's so new to me," Jill said, shivering and wrapping her towel tightly around her. "Lob shots, bounce shots, power shots, slap shots—and all those offensive plays. Whew! No wonder Malcolm keeps griping at us to take the game more seriously!"

Malcolm was standing at the sidelines, now, calling out new instructions every minute to one player or another. He was really getting on their nerves, Jill could tell.

So she wasn't very surprised when, after the last whistle had been blown, Paul came creeping up behind Malcolm. "We won, Malcolm," he called out with enthusiasm. "Are you proud of us?"

"Indeed I am," Malcolm said, but his face didn't look proud. "But the score might have been even higher if only you'd all listened to me—"

"Too bad you never wear your bathing suit, Mal," Paul said. There was an evil gleam in his eye. "I mean, here you are at the pool with all your clothes on."

Malcolm suddenly looked worried. "Paul, don't you dare—"

"Sorry, dear old Prez," someone called from in the pool. "We took a vote just now, and since we're the victorious team we think you owe us one."

Paul gave Malcolm a gentle shove, and he went tumbling into the pool, clothes and all. A shout of joy rang out among all the Rosemont club members. "We did it!" someone yelled. "We finally did it!"

The Morris fans cheered from their bleachers, too.

"Mal looks like a fish out of water, even when he's *in* the water," Paul said, laughing.

Jill turned her head, trying to hide a smile. And she saw Terrence standing beside her. He had the most maddening way of appearing at her side constantly.

"Hope they don't throw me in," he said. "I'm practically the only other person here not in a bathing suit!"

"I wouldn't let them," Suzie piped up, appearing beside him and putting her arm through his. "I think I have some influence around this club."

Terrence didn't have to worry about it. The players seemed to be overjoyed now that they'd gotten their revenge on Malcolm. And it turned out that Paul had even brought along extra clothes, cadged from Malcolm's roommate, so that the president wouldn't have to go home in the cold air soaking wet.

"Now you've gone too far. You're getting much too rowdy," Malcolm complained as he stepped out of the pool, sloshing water with each step. His glasses were still on, but were askew on his face, and his shirt and pants oozed water. "I suppose you think that things like this are funny. Well, I have a good mind to resign—"

He stared at Terrence, who he knew was a reporter from the paper. "But that's probably what they want," Malcolm said. "And if I were gone, the whole club would fall apart. I just know it. So I guess I'll stay."

"Maybe you ought to wear your bathing suit from now on, Malcolm," Terrence advised him. Terrence was trying hard to keep a straight face. But it wasn't easy.

Riding back to Rosemont, Terrence was once again in the seat beside Jill. And she felt just as uncomfortable as she had on the trip to Morris. She was attracted to him, and it was maddening. How could she be interested in Terrence, even slightly, when she was already in love with Ryan Davis?

It didn't make any sense. Jill had gone out only with Craig for such a long time, and now here she was wavering back and forth between two completely different types of guys.

Was it being away at college that was causing this vast change in her? she wondered. Or could it be that she was just intrigued by the differences between Terrence and the mysterious Ryan? She sighed. She didn't know what to think anymore.

The victory party was held at Pasta Heaven, the pizza place just on the outskirts of town. The club chose it because it had a small dance floor and a jukebox full of good rock.

"Not to mention the world's second-best pizza," Suzie told Terrence as they entered the large, dimly lit restaurant. Suzie was sticking to him like glue, Jill noticed. "Weird Willie's has the world-class best pizza, of course."

136

"Of course," Terrence agreed and winked in Jill's direction.

They sat around a long table close to the dance floor. Malcolm did the ordering, managing to sound very self-important, and the club members gave him the floor. They were happy now, Jill noticed, because they had had their little joke with him.

The players were starving after their strenuous match. Pizza after pizza arrived at the table and each was gobbled up immediately. Soon the group began to attract the attention of the other patrons in the restaurant.

"They must think we're complete hogs," Jill whispered to Terrence and Suzie.

"So what?" Suzie said, shrugging. "Maybe we are!" She licked her fingers and continued devouring her pepperoni and mushroom slice.

Finally, their appetites appeased, the club members cheered and Paul stood up to make a speech.

"To show that we really love you, Malcolm, and in hopes that you'll forgive us for dunking you, we all chipped in to buy you a special gift."

Malcolm opened the package, looking very suspicious. But he appeared to be pleased when he held up his new T-shirt and read the message on its front: "I'm Their Leader. Which Way Did They Go?"

Then some of the members began to get up to dance.

"You'll dance with me, won't you, Terrence?" Suzie asked purringly. And without giving him a chance to object, she led him off to the dance floor. Jill sat there and tried not to watch as the two of them moved to the beat of the Billy Joel record.

She saw them out of the corner of her eye— Suzie small and blond, bouncy and animated, and Terrence tall and strong, his face devoid of much expression. Suzie kept throwing her head back, laughing and giving her partner admiring glances.

He's only human, Jill thought. *He could fall for Suzie, just because she's so persistent. And so full of life.*

Everybody seems to be part of a couple except me, she suddenly thought dismally. *I lost Craig. I couldn't get Ryan interested . . .*

She stabbed the straw into her soda, sloshing ice cubes around in her glass.

And Terrence? she thought. *Maybe I'm letting a really good guy slip out of my hands and right into Suzie's.*

Just then Malcolm, of all people, cut in on Suzie and Terrence. Jill heard him say, "Suzie, you got away with pinching my cheeks earlier." He was grinning. "So I'm going to claim you for this dance."

Suzie turned white, but she managed to smile graciously as she was whirled away by Malcolm.

Terrence returned to the table but didn't sit down.

"That Suzie is quite a girl," he commented. "Have you ever seen such a flirt before?"

Jill stared at him. "You ought to be flattered. She doesn't flirt with just anybody, I'm sure. She likes you."

Terrence met her gaze with his calm, honest green eyes. "Well, I happen to like *you*," he said quietly. "Will you dance with me, Jill?"

She did get up to dance with Terrence, because she was curious about herself—and him. And the experience was every bit as upsetting as sitting near him on the bus had been.

Terrence held her firmly but not tightly. He was an accomplished dancer, she realized right away. He was a sociable, cheerful person and had, no doubt, been popular back in whatever high school he came from. Terrence was no amateur when it came to girls.

Jill breathed in the scent of him and felt her pulse quicken. That wonderful after-shave-and-soap combination—who *did* it remind her of?

She put her head back and tried to make conversation. "I guess you'll have enough information for a good article for the *Voice*, won't you?"

"Jill," Terrence said patiently, "I don't want to talk about writing right now. Okay?" He pulled her closer, just a fraction closer, but enough to make her feel a little dizzy.

She forced herself to relax, trying to enjoy the music and the feeling that she had being in Terrence's arms. *Strong arms*, she thought with surprise. *Just like someone else's* . . .

The dance floor was dark, and Jill felt, for a moment, as though she and Terrence were all alone in the world. So when he stopped dancing, she knew instinctively what he was going to do.

He leaned over without ceremony and kissed her. He kissed her softly, not with insistence. His lips felt firm and warm, and somehow familiar.

"I've been wanting to do that for a long time, Jill," he said. "Hope I'm not out of line."

"No," she said dreamily. "You're not."

The second kiss was even warmer and more wonderful. Jill pressed closer to him, sliding her arms up around his neck as their lips met again.

Everything was perfect. They were wrapped in their own dark little cocoon, insulated from the entire world. They fit together perfectly, as though they'd been dancing and kissing all their lives.

"Oh, Craig—" Jill whispered before she realized what she was saying.

"Craig?"

The magic moment was shattered. Terrence stiffened and pulled back, looking more than a little annoyed. Jill, for her part, was horrified.

"Oh, I'm so sorry," she said quickly, stammering. "I didn't mean—I mean, I forgot—I don't know how I could have—"

Terrence was staring at her with disbelief. And hurt, of course; oh, yes, she could see that he was terribly hurt.

"I don't know what made me say that. Oh, my gosh. I feel terrible about this—"

"Well, so do I, as a matter of fact." Terrence ran his fingers through his hair, and his face looked drawn and pale. "Here I thought we were making some sort of progress, and now—"

"I know. This is unforgivable," Jill sputtered. "Let me think, Terrence, please. Let me think."

Terrence sighed and pulled her off into deeper shadows, away from the dance floor. "Jill, I've been patient for this long, so, of course, I can be patient for a little longer." But his foot began to tap with a rhythm that definitely showed his impatience.

"Anything wrong?" Suzie called out in a sweet voice as she and Malcolm danced nearby. "You two aren't dancing. Gosh, Jill, if playing water polo made you that exhausted, maybe you ought to turn Terrence over to me."

"She's such a flirt!" Jill muttered, so low that only Terrence could hear. Tears filled her eyes. "I suppose you're thinking you'd be better off with Suzie, now," Jill said with a groan.

Terrence put his arms around Jill. "Maybe," he whispered. "Maybe not. I just wish I could understand you, Jill."

Jill watched the way Terrence's mouth moved, and the way his eyes sparkled in the dim light. That was it! His face once again triggered the feeling of déjà vu she'd had every time she looked at him!

"Terrence," she said slowly, "I believe I *do* know why I said Craig's name. I think I've just figured it out."

"Well, please let me in on it."

"You look a little bit like Craig—handsome and tall. Your personality is a lot like his—funny, relaxed. Oh, Terrence, I honestly didn't realize it, but *all this time* you've been reminding me of him!"

"Is that good or bad?"

"I'm not sure. I was trying to avoid you, Terrence, because something inside me kept saying, 'Don't get hurt again!' But tonight, when we were close and dancing so perfectly together, it was just as if—" She stopped.

"Just as if you were back with Craig again," Terrence finished for her. "The boy you really love."

Jill hung her head. "I don't know about that. I really don't know!" She was so ashamed and so confused.

"I think I understand, Jill," he said quietly. "It wasn't me you were kissing at all. It was Craig."

"Yes, but that's so terrible of me! Maybe— maybe I haven't gotten over him yet," she said lamely. "I thought I was doing just great—" She felt utterly miserable about hurting Terrence.

"Don't get so upset about it, Jill," Terrence said. Then he did a surprising thing. He brushed his lips across her forehead in a very gentle way. "Mistakes like this happen. People do remind us of other people. It happens all the time."

"Oh, but I've been so stupid, and so blind—"

"No. You've been confused, and that's a normal human condition. I guess I've got to learn to give you more time, that's all."

"I suppose so, but—" Words failed her. She wasn't sure what she wanted to say, exactly.

SIXTEEN

"I think I've decided to become an old maid, Cassie," Jill told her roommate later that night.

Cassie didn't even look up from the book she was absorbed in. "Oh? That's interesting."

"No, I mean it." Jill was staring at herself in the mirror, holding a brush in her hand but not showing much interest in brushing her hair. Her throat was hurting, and her spirits were definitely sagging.

"You hate men, huh?" Cassie said.

"It's not that I hate them. But I have such awful, rotten luck with them, Cassie." Jill turned to see if Cassandra was listening to her at all. She got the definite feeling that nothing was going to pull Cassie's attention away from her book.

If only Toni were here, Jill thought sadly. Toni always listened to her problems and took them seriously—especially when they were boy problems. After all, to Toni, boy problems were really the only kind worth having.

Even though Cassie had admitted that she was basically shy and that she wished she could fall in

143

love, Jill didn't think that Cassie would be sympathetic to her tale of woe as far as boys were concerned.

Jill wished she had enough quarters to call Toni again, but she didn't, so that settled that. Instead, she turned to the mirror again and began to talk to herself.

"Well, if anyone catches me doing this, they'll think I'm a true sick-o, but I'm going to talk to *you*, Jill Gardner. You, there, with that dumb expression on your face!"

Cassandra mumbled, her head still buried in her book.

"You had two perfectly nice friends, Jill," Jill went on, pointing a finger at her own reflection. "Ryan was willing to be your friend, but what did you do? You went chasing after him like a maniac. And why? All because you were afraid of being *alone*. As soon as Craig broke up with you, you let yourself develop a crush on him—an older man."

She stopped. That was the problem, wasn't it? Maybe she'd been flinging herself at Ryan just because he was older and hard to get. And where was he now? Nowhere, that's where.

"And Terrence?" she went on angrily. "You had a real nice friend there. In fact, he'd have made a wonderful boy to date, if only you'd given him a chance. You probably could have gone to all the college dances with him, maybe even the Thanksgiving dance. But what did you do?"

"Huh? I didn't do anything," Cassandra muttered.

Jill sighed deeply and continued to address the mirror. "You know what you did, Jill. I won't even discuss it. You know exactly what your subconscious mind did, and how you hurt poor Terrence so much that he probably won't even consider being your friend anymore."

"What's that?" Cassie asked, suddenly looking up. "You did something to hurt Terrence?"

"Never mind," Jill said wearily. "None of it matters anyway. I just plan on living the rest of my life all alone as a spinster." She reached down and patted Jelly Bean. "I'll probably have a dozen or so cats to keep me from feeling too lonely."

"Now that's a good idea," said Cassandra, looking up with interest. "Cats are always the solution to one's problems. Besides, if you think you've got it rough, then how about this character in my book, Raskolnikov, who's being shipped off to Siberia?"

"Well, at least she knows where she's heading," Jill said miserably.

"He. Raskolnikov's a he. Hey, Jill, are you feeling all right? You really look pale."

"I'm fine," Jill said. But, in truth, she wasn't feeling up to par. Ever since Saturday when she'd gotten caught in the rain with Ryan, she'd been fighting off a chest cold. And now her throat was really sore, too.

145

"Maybe you ought to go to the infirmary, Jill." Cassandra got up and pulled a thermometer out of her dresser drawer. "My mother made me bring this—do you believe it?" Cassandra kept talking as she washed the instrument carefully in the bathroom sink. "I don't believe in being a hypochondriac, but maybe this will come in handy right now."

"Oh, Cassie, I don't need—" But Jill was silenced by the thermometer being thrust under her tongue.

"Shush. I heard you sneezing and coughing a few times last night," Cassandra said. "You know there's been some flu going around. No, don't say a word—just keep your mouth closed so we can check your temp."

Cassandra grinned. "I sound like a nurse or a doctor, don't I? Maybe that's what I should be taking—premed courses. Or, better yet, I could be a vet and use all my skills on animals. Or I could go back to India to help the people in remote villages."

Jill made a gurgling sound behind tightly closed lips.

"You know, that's not such a bad idea," Cassandra mused. "I've never been able to find anything that I really wanted to study—except literature, and I couldn't stand to teach."

She put a professional hand on Jill's forehead. "How would I look as a doctor? Can't you just see me with a white jacket and a stethoscope?"

Jill nodded.

Cassandra laughed at herself. "No, of course you can't. But you have given me something to think about, Jill."

"Uuumm?" Jill managed to say, pointing at herself.

"Yeah. And wouldn't my father go crazy with joy if I went into medicine?" Cassie's face clouded over suddenly. "Of course my mother would never go for it. She'd rather see me *marry* a doctor or a vet than be one."

But Jill, still unable to talk, thought that Cassandra was on to a good thing. She could imagine her friend with a medical degree, working efficiently and deftly in some vet's office or in India. She'd be great, Jill thought. And she vowed to discuss the idea with Cassie soon.

Finally the thermometer was removed. "You're running a temp, Jill. I really think you should go to the health office right now."

"No," Jill said tiredly. "It's just a cold, Cassie, and I think a good night's sleep will take care of it."

"Famous freshman last words," Cassie said.

"What?"

"I mean that plenty of freshmen get sick— really sick—because they don't know enough to take care of themselves when they get away from home. Admit it. What would your mother be doing for you right now, if you were at home?"

"Oh, gosh, she'd have the vitamin C out and the aspirin, and probably some cough syrup and the Vicks to rub on my chest."

"Yes, the whole treatment. And she'd probably make you stay in bed for a day or two, wouldn't she?"

"I can't do that," Jill protested. "Not at college, no way! The classes are hard enough, without missing any! I'd never, never cut classes—"

"But when you're sick, Jill, that's different."

"No." Jill was sounding emphatic. "I just can't stay in bed. I might skip water polo practice for a while, but I've got to go to classes."

Cassandra was glaring at her angrily. And then she gave one of her characteristic shrugs of indifference, retreating back to her old self. "Do whatever you want," she said flatly. "You always do anyway."

"Oh, Cassie, don't be so grumpy!" Jill begged. "I really do thank you for your concern—and I think you'd make an excellent doctor or vet, you know, I really do."

"Forget it."

"No, Cassie, I think it's a really good idea."

"Forget it," Cassie grumbled, putting her nose back into *Crime and Punishment*.

And Jill knew that their little moment of closeness was over. Not that she cared much, anyway, right then. She was beginning to feel worse and worse every minute.

I think I'll skip my homework tonight, she thought, *and get some sleep*. She changed wearily into her pajamas and barely made it into bed. She was asleep the moment her head touched the pillow.

148

SEVENTEEN

The next morning Jill couldn't even lift her head from the pillow. She felt sick all over, as though someone had whacked every part of her body with a giant sledgehammer.

"Oh," she groaned just as Cassandra was getting ready to leave for an early class. "Wait a minute. I think I need help."

Cassandra came over to Jill's bed and placed the competent doctor's hand back on her forehead. "You *are* burning up, now," she pronounced. "Jill, this could be serious. You aren't going to argue with me anymore, are you, about going to the infirmary?"

"No," Jill moaned. "The only problem is, how do I *get* there? I feel too weak to walk."

"Stay right where you are. I think I can get someone to help, and then you'll be all set—" Cassandra dashed out of the room. It was unusual for Cassandra to be in such a hurry. Generally she moved in a slow, deliberate way.

"Who's coming to help?" Jill asked when Cassandra returned. "Heather? Marcie? Robert? Jason? Who?"

"Now just you worry about getting yourself ready. Do you want to get dressed or go in your pajamas?"

"Dressed, I suppose. Oh, who cares? I doubt if I can get up the strength to put a leg into my jeans."

"Yes, you can," Cassandra told her as she helped her don her various articles of clothing. Jill was so limp that she could hardly lift her arms to slip them into her sweatshirt.

"I knew you were letting this cold thing go too long," Cassandra muttered. "I feel responsible. I shouldn't have let you get away with it! And, yes, I know—I probably sound just like your mother!"

"More like my doctor. Or vet." Jill managed a weak smile. She felt a surge of gratitude for having this extra special roommate. Cassie liked to pretend that she didn't care about anyone, but in reality she could be just as caring about people as she was about animals, Jill realized as Cassandra pulled her jumbled hair into a hasty ponytail.

Just as they managed to get Jill's sneakers on her feet, there was a knock on the door. "Come in," Cassandra called.

Jill almost fell over when she saw who entered the room. It was Terrence!

"Hi, girls. I came as fast as I could. I'm glad you called me, Cassandra." He walked over to the side of the bed. "Oh, you look terrible, Jill."

"Thanks," she said weakly.

"But we'll get you over to the infirmary one way or another."

"Thanks for coming, Terrence," Cassandra said. "I kept trying to think of the strongest person around, and you were the one who came to mind."

"I can handle it, even if I have to carry her all the way."

"No, no. I plan to help, too," Cassandra said. "One of us on each side of her. Okay—ready, Jill? Here we go."

As they hoisted her up, Robert peeked in the door. "You know, you could probably call campus security to take her," he informed them.

"I don't think so," Cassandra said. "Then everybody at Rosemont might think Jill was being arrested for something. Another food fight, maybe."

Jill smiled weakly. "And you're the one who always says you don't care what people think."

"I don't." Cassandra and Terrence managed to give Jill a good heave to get her down the front steps of the McGregor porch. "But I suppose I might care if they said something about *you*."

About halfway there Jill protested that she had to sit down for just a second. "I have to rest," she gasped. "I can't—I don't think I can go another step."

Terrence was looking at her worriedly. "I could carry her," he said. "Or we could call a security car—but I think I see something that's easier and quicker!"

He ducked behind some trees and went around the gardener's shed. When he returned he was pushing a giant wheelbarrow.

"Here you are, ma'am. Rickshaw service, made to order."

Jill's eyes popped out in disbelief. So did Cassandra's, for a moment, and then she began to laugh uproariously.

"You're all right, Terrence," Cassie said. "I like a person who uses his brain."

"How about me?" Jill asked. "What if I don't feel like riding in a richshaw?" But she knew she was too weak to argue, and anyway the wheelbarrow looked like a blessing suddenly. She could sink into it and not have to lift her head or move another muscle.

"This is okay, after all," she told them as they crunched through fallen autumn leaves toward the infirmary. "Thank you, Terrence. And you, too, Cassie."

"Never mind, Jill. Just keep quiet and save your strength."

Jill was aware that every passerby was doing a double take at the sight of her curled up in the wheelbarrow.

"Boy, that must have been some party!" one boy commented.

"It was," Cassandra said with utter aplomb. "Too bad you missed it."

"Looks like you're a mighty sick little lady," the doctor told Jill a short while later.

"I'm not a little lady," she tried to say, but the words didn't really come out loud enough to be heard. She was feeling dizzy and seemed to be slipping in and out of consciousness.

"Looks like flu. And near-pneumonia," she heard the doctor telling the infirmary nurse. "Let's get her into an isolation room and start administering antibiotics right away."

Isolation room? *No*, Jill thought drowsily. She hated isolation of any kind, especially when she was sick! But it didn't seem to matter what she wanted. She was put on a hospital gurney and wheeled out of the examining room.

Terrence and Cassie were in the outer office, looking worried.

"She'll be in isolation for a while," they were told by the nurse. "Are you her roommate?" Cassie nodded. "Will you call her parents? Tell them, please, to get in touch with me, Miss Armbruster. I'll be her nurse for the next week or so."

"Yes, ma'am," Cassandra promised. Jill noticed that both Cassie and Terrence were looking at the big, sour-faced nurse as though they couldn't believe their eyes.

Miss Armbruster was not only big and beefy, but she had a voice like a foghorn.

"She looks and sounds like a top sergeant," Cassandra whispered to Terrence and Jill when the nurse was preoccupied elsewhere.

Terrence squeezed Jill's hand. "Get well, okay?"

Jill moaned. The fever was making her delirious. "I don't want Suzie to get you," she murmured before she could stop herself. "I'd really miss you if you were in love with Suzie—"

Terrence smiled broadly.

"Don't worry," he said. There was a happy note in his voice. "You just worry about getting well. I don't give up that easily, Jill."

EIGHTEEN

"First time anybody's ever arrived at this infirmary in a wheelbarrow," clucked Miss Armbruster as she wheeled Jill into the isolation room on the first floor, which was the girls' section of the small hospital. "Highly unsanitary, if you ask me."

No sense of humor, Jill thought, wondering what kind of a stay she was in for with this nurse.

"Wheelbarrow, indeed!" the nurse went on, harrumphing as she helped Jill undress and put on a hospital gown. "Well, I'm used to taking care of college kids. Don't expect to have any visitors, young lady. Not while you're this sick. Heaven knows what those friends of yours might try to pull next!"

Jill didn't protest. She was glad to be settled into the cool sheets of the hospital bed, after her bumpy wheelbarrow ride.

But suddenly a wave of homesickness washed over her. She hated it there in that sterile white hospital room! She wanted her mother, and she

155

wanted her own bed, back in Seattle. She wanted her mother's comforting presence. "Now you just rest, Jill darling, and you'll start to feel better in no time." And she wanted a big bowl of her mother's homemade chicken soup, the kind with the noodles.

I don't want to be away from home when I'm sick, she thought miserably and childishly. *I want . . . I want . . .* Luckily, she was too weak to stay awake long to dwell on these things.

For those first two days it didn't really matter where Jill was. She was asleep most of the time, and whenever she did wake up she took her medicine, received her sponge baths, and conked right out again. The young doctor who had admitted her appeared from time to time, but she was never certain whether he really was there or not. Everything seemed to float around her as if in a dream. She coughed and ached and slept and dreamed.

The only absolute reality was Miss Armbruster—the sergeant. And she managed to make things worse by coming in quite often with the message, "Your mother called again. She calls every day to see how you're doing. She sends her love and says get well." Then, seeing the pained look on Jill's face, she'd add, kindly, "There, there, dear. I know you wish you could talk to her yourself. But there's time for that later."

Adjusting the window shade, the nurse said, "There's also some very demanding person named

Toni who keeps calling. Keeps insisting that she talk to you. I had to tell her that was impossible!"

By Thursday Jill was awake enough to sit up and eat a breakfast of soft-boiled eggs, juice, and toast. She actually felt like eating for the first time since she'd been admitted.

She looked around the room for the first time, too. She was amazed to see that flowers had been delivered at some point.

"Can I get up to see the flowers and the cards?" she dared to ask Miss Armbruster.

"Absolutely not" was the firm reply. "You don't leave that bed for another whole day. Not until Dr. Walker says you're well enough to make a bathroom trip. And then, only with me helping you."

"Things must be slow here in the infirmary," Jill said, thinking that the nurse shouldn't have so much time to devote to her alone.

"We have a few patients up on the boys' ward, but you're my only charge on this floor. Now. If you want to read the cards, I'll bring them to you."

Miss Armbruster collected the small white florist cards and deposited them on Jill's bedside tray.

The first card, taken from the largest bouquet of roses, was from her parents. "Get well, darling," it said, and Jill felt a large lump forming in her throat when she thought of her mother dictating that message to some florist back in Seattle. "All our love, Mother and Dad."

157

ON OUR OWN

The second one, a bunch of cheerful daisies, was from Terrence. The card read, "Love, Terrence."

An unusual display of irises and some exotic flowers Jill didn't even recognize stood towering over the other bouquets. It was beautiful, and it was from Cassandra. The card said, "From your roomie. I miss you here. So does Jelly Bean."

There were roses in a tall vase from "Russel and all the staff of the *Voice*." Jill felt flattered by this tribute. There was a teddy bear–shaped planter with an African violet plant, and the card on that said, "What's going on? Get well quick! Luv, luv, luv, Toni."

And the final card, which came with a glossy philodendron, was signed, "Get well—From your water polo buddies!"

Jill was greatly cheered by all these messages. She hadn't realized that she had that many good friends at Rosemont. Then Ryan flashed through her thoughts, and she wished that there had been a get-well card from him, but he probably didn't even know that she was sick.

"Will I be able to talk to any of my friends or family on the phone?" she asked Miss Armbruster, who was busy snapping sheets in preparation for changing the bed.

"Not until Dr. Walker lets you leave this room," the nurse said. "There are no phones in the isolation rooms. We don't want our very sick patients being bothered by a lot of nonsense calls!"

Jill wanted to ask just how sick she was, but she saved the question for Dr. Walker, who appeared later that day.

"Welcome back to the world," he said, smiling at Jill. He was a pleasant young doctor with a trim mustache and intelligent-looking blue eyes. "I'm glad to hear that you ate most of your breakfast."

"I'm starting to feel better, Doctor," Jill assured him. "I was wondering—Miss Armbruster seems to think I can't leave this bed. Am I that terribly sick?"

"You have been, Jill, but you're certainly on the road to recovery now. However, I'd like to see you stay right there for the next twenty-four hours except to get up to use the bathroom. You're going to have dizzy spells if you try to move around too quickly."

"You mean I'm never going to get to leave this room?" Jill was beginning to feel as though a prison sentence had been placed on her.

"For a while." The doctor smiled knowingly. "All our kids want to get loose so they can find the pay phone and get in touch with their friends. And that's usually a bad idea. I think if you have any messages to send, you can write a few notes, and Miss Armbruster will see that your friends are notified."

"Oh, great." Jill sank back on her pile of pillows and pouted.

"That act won't work with me," Dr. Walker said with a big amused smile. "I've had a few years' experience now. I've learned to harden my heart."

"Why do you want to be so hardhearted, at such a young age?" Jill argued, but the doctor only laughed out loud.

"Bed rest," he ordered firmly. He headed for the door. "And, by the way, I have to say this, that wheelbarrow trick was the greatest entrance I've ever seen!" Still chuckling, he left the room.

Jill couldn't help laughing along with him. Her trip across campus *had* been unique. At least she'd have an interesting topic to write about for her next column.

But in the meantime, this staying in bed was going to be intolerable, she thought. No visitors? No telephone? Unthinkable!

When that monster woman came back, she'd ask for notepaper and try to dash off a few words to her friends. But in the meantime she had nothing to look forward to but sheer boredom.

There was a tapping at the window.

Jill brightened immediately. Had Cassie somehow managed to climb up the fire escape, to appear at her window? That would be super, she thought.

But no. Oddly enough, there was a Dixie cup tapping at her window. Jill blinked once, and then again, to be sure she was seeing correctly. Why was there a Dixie cup bobbing out there in the middle of space? Was she still feverish and having hallucinations?

Squinting her eyes, she saw that a string was holding the cup there, a string that extended up beyond the top of the window. *It must be from upstairs*, she thought and remembered something about the boys' ward being above her.

"Bed rest, huh?" she said out loud and gingerly swung her legs over the side of the bed. She was going to find out what that Dixie cup was doing there!

She managed to stagger over to the window, but immediately she was aware that the doctor had been right: she *was* weak and dizzy and really shouldn't be up at all.

"Oh, just don't let me faint," she said breathily as she clutched at the windowsill. She managed to give the window a small shove and reached out carefully to the paper cup.

Just as she'd hoped. There was a note in the cup!

"What are you doing out of bed?!" The booming voice bellowed across the room at her, making her almost drop the precious note. But she managed to hold on to it and wad it up tightly in her fist so that Miss Armbruster wouldn't see it.

"I—just needed a little air," she lied. "And now I really am feeling faint—"

"Of course you are!" The woman was at her side in a flash, and in all the commotion of holding Jill upright, she failed to see the dangling Dixie cup outside the window. *Thank heavens*, Jill thought. If the nurse had seen it, she would no doubt have reported it to someone on the floor above.

"You get back into this bed and you stay there!" Miss Armbruster ordered, taking Jill firmly by the arm and propelling her toward the bed. "Needed fresh air, indeed! If you try that again, miss, you won't be getting any of your messages."

"My messages?"

"Yes. There have been a few notes for you, dropped off at my office. I'll bring them in to you in about an hour, if you can behave yourself."

"Oh, I will," Jill said fervently.

"And, of course, your mother called again. She sends her love." Miss Armbruster sounded as though she approved of mothers getting in touch with her patients. But to Jill it was a stab in the heart because she longed to hear her mother's voice for herself.

Finally the sergeant left the room, and Jill was able to uncrumple the piece of paper from the Dixie cup.

"Hello down there," said the note in a bold male handwriting. "If there's anybody alive anywhere in the world, please have pity on a feverish patient. I'm so isolated up here I think I'm in Siberia."

Jill had to smile. She had been feeling the exact same way!

The note went on: "If you are alive please drop me a note in return. Give a tug on the Dixie cup, and I'll know."

That was all. But to Jill it was enough. It was proof that someone else existed somewhere in the hospital, and that someone was just as lonely as she was.

She found a pen in her bedside drawer, but the only paper she could come up with was a dinner napkin. Good enough for now, she thought, and she began to write an answer to the boy upstairs.

Dear Dixie cup friend,
      Yes, I am alive but only just barely. They've just saved me from the brink of death, if I'm to believe my very, very strict nurse. I don't know how I'll be able to get this message over to the window, to tell you the truth, but I'll have to give it a try. You sound as desolate as I feel. What's wrong with you? I've had the flu, I guess.

Before she had a chance to write any more or even sign her name, Jill was surprised to see the woman from the housekeeping department come in. And this gave her an idea.

"Am I ever glad to see you!" Jill said. "You look like the friendly type, even if nobody else is around here."

The woman, middle-aged and small, laughed heartily. "You must be having the usual troubles with Miss Armbruster," she said shrewdly. "All the kids feel the same way. She making your life miserable?"

"Yes. And I need help with something."

The woman leaned on her mop handle and stared at Jill, looking very jolly and pleasant. "Okay," she said simply. "What can I do for you?"

Jill explained about the Dixie cup, and the woman, who said her name was Mollie, offered to place Jill's note in the cup.

"I love to put one over on Miss Armbruster," Mollie declared gleefully. She put the unsigned note into the cup and gave it a tug. "Darned if you college kids don't think of everything! I never saw the likes of that before."

"Whoever's up there is pretty smart," Jill conceded. "Do you clean upstairs? Do you know who's there?"

Mollie just smiled. "That would be tellin', wouldn't it?" she said mysteriously. And Jill could learn nothing further from Mollie.

But she was grateful that the note had been sent, because the Dixie cup did disappear for a while. When it came back again, tapping at the windowpane, Mollie was just finishing up the floor mopping.

"There's your boyfriend callin'." Mollie reached out for the note and handed it to Jill. "Well, I've got to be on my way. See you tomorrow."

"Thanks so much, for everything."

Jill waited until she was gone before she opened the note.

Hello again, fellow prisoner!

It warms my heart to know that someone else shares my miserable fate. At least we can make the dreary hours fly faster if we correspond—*n'est-ce pas*? I see you didn't sign your name. Good. I think it would be special to remain secret pals and never divulge our names. Do you agree?

Dixie Cup Dan

Jill laughed out loud. This was so much fun!

NINETEEN

Miss Armbruster came in with Jill's lunch, a pile of messages from the outside world, and some blank notepaper.

"And you're to eat every bit of this lunch, do you hear?" said the nurse.

"Liver? Yuck." Jill made a face, but she knew it wouldn't do her much good. She was stuck with a meal of fried liver, lots of nutritious spinach, and a mound of mashed potatoes that would choke a horse. "Er—I'm really not terribly hungry," she added. "But, of course, I'll give it a try."

Satisfied with that, Miss Armbruster left the room. Jill ignored the food on her tray and opened her notes.

The first was from Cassandra.

Hey, Jill, I hope this note gets past the Armbruster and you're able to read it. She tells us you're recovering. Fever gone, appetite back. Glad to hear it. As I said on the card with the flowers, Jelly Bean and I sure miss you.

Anything I can get for you, or do for you, while you're in there? I called your folks, and they were going to notify your friend Toni.

I also went to all your professors to explain your absence. They're compiling a list of your assignments so that when you're able, you can sit up there in bed and do your homework. Knowing you, that'll make you feel much better about things.

You'll never guess what else I did. When I went to tell your water polo captain why you wouldn't be at practice, he corralled me and wanted to know if I could substitute for you! Paul, that is, not Malcolm. That Paul certainly is persuasive. And rather cute, in his own way.

Well, aside from that—I did end up playing a practice game with the group. And I wasn't bad! I hope you don't mind. I'd never try to take your place, you know that, but I thought filling in would be okay with you. Is it?

Jill smiled when she read that. She couldn't imagine Cassandra joining in any organized sport voluntarily. But Jill was very pleased about it. After all, she'd been worrying about Cassie, thinking it was unnatural that she never allowed herself contact with anyone other than representatives of an animal-welfare group.

Jill closed her eyes and tried to picture Cassandra in the pool, swatting at the water polo ball in one of those tight ugly caps. She had to suppress a giggle.

Then she revised the picture and visualized Cassandra trying to get Paul's attention because she found him so "cute." Now there was a possibility. Paul was very different from Cassie, but what was that they said about opposites attracting? She'd often thought that when Cassandra met just the right boy, she would tumble pretty hard! Maybe this was the beginning of something.

Cassandra's note went on, "I notified Ryan Davis, of course, because he's Professor Blake's T.A., that you were in the infirmary. He seemed very worried and said he'd help you keep up with the psych class notes.

"Anyway, get well quickly and let me know what you need from your room. I'll just fill up a wheelbarrow and tote it all over! Love, Cassie."

Jill sighed. She reread the part about Ryan and wished that her heart didn't flip-flop every time his name was mentioned. Why did she have to be in love with an older man who didn't have a romantic bone in his body?

The note from Russel, the newspaper editor, was short.

Don't worry about your column for a while, Jill. Just concentrate on getting well. The paper is unusually short-handed this week, and we miss you and your humorous words, but we'd rather see you save your strength for getting better.

Best wishes, Russel

The last note was from Terrence.

Dear Jill,
Sorry about the wheelbarrow, but it was the only thing I could think to do on such short notice. I guess you really did create a sensation on the Rosemont campus. People have been talking about it for days.

I miss you and want to see you well, really soon. Maybe I handled things badly that night at the pizza parlor. I came on too strong, and it wasn't your fault that I reminded you of—that person I remind you of.

Please think of me now and then. I check with the sergeant twice a day to find out your progress, in case she hasn't told you.

Love, Terrence

Jill smiled. She was feeling better now that all these notes had arrived.

Maybe I have carved out a little place for myself here at Rosemont, she thought with pride. She certainly had a bunch of good friends now, and that was a comforting thought.

And let's not forget my secret pal, she thought. She owed him a letter now.

But first she had to find a way to choke down that fried liver!

Dear Secret Pal,

Having just forced myself to swallow some dry, overcooked liver, I am tempted to ask, "Is that what they served you, too? Or is it just a special torture that Miss Armbruster has reserved for *me*?"

Tell me more about yourself. I find myself curious, even though I agree that we remain "secret pals." So—no names. But you can tell me what you're like, can't you?

Best wishes,
Your First Floor Secret Pal

Somehow Jill managed to sneak to the window to reach for the Dixie cup without being caught by Miss Armbruster. She realized that she was stronger, too, and didn't feel as dizzy as before.

Guess all that liver really helps, she thought wryly.

She tugged on the string and scooted back into bed. When the nurse appeared next, Jill was sitting there looking as innocent as a newborn baby.

"Hmmm," said Miss Armbruster. "Don't know if I trust that angelic look on your face, young lady. You been up to something?"

"No, of course not," lied Jill. "I'm just happy because I heard from my friends. Thanks for giving me my letters."

"Hmmmph. You're welcome, of course." Miss Armbruster began to collect the things on Jill's lunch tray. "Well, you can write back to them; I'll see that they get the notes. But be sure you stay right in this bed!"

Jill smiled sweetly. "Oh, of course, I will."

But, of course, Jill didn't. The next time the Dixie cup appeared at her window she was up in a flash.

Dear Secret Pal,

This corresponding is a lifesaver for me. You have no idea. Well, what can I tell you about me? That I am an incurable homicidal maniac? That I am the official campus cat burglar, at times? Or that I am the sole reason for the high rate of professorial burnout and the cause of many a fine teacher leaving this revered institution?

Does that tell you something about me?

And now what about you? Please tell me all, except your name, of course. I'm wildly curious about you.

Hope you'll answer.

Dixie Cup Dan

Jill laughed out loud when she read the note, and she remembered hearing somewhere that laughter was absolutely the best way to recover from a serious illness. In that case, her secret pal was the most excellent medicine that could be prescribed.

Her nurse didn't hold to that theory, however. She charged into the room. "What's the laughing about? We can't have that. You'll aggravate your cough again."

"Yes, Miss Armbruster," Jill said as meekly as she could and stuffed the secret pal letter down under her blankets.

"Pneumonia is no joke, you know," warned the nurse as she popped a thermometer into Jill's mouth. "We have to keep a close watch on you for any signs of a relapse."

"Uumph," Jill replied.

Jill wrote notes to all her friends on Friday. She thanked Cassie for all she'd done and added just one P.S. "Please, will you tell Ryan Davis again how sick I've been? I find it hard to believe that he wouldn't even send me a get-well card. I can't help thinking about him all the time."

You're a fool, Jill Gardner, she told herself after she'd written that to Cassandra. *You might as well be asking her to notify Craig! He couldn't care less whether you're dead or alive.*

She wrote to her parents, trying to make her illness sound like nothing more than a cold, and she wrote a short thank-you note to Terrence, telling him the daisies were beautiful.

And now she was getting tired. *I'll write to Toni tomorrow,* she thought wearily. Her eyes were growing heavy, and she knew that a nap was inevitable for her.

"What day *is* tomorrow, anyway?" she asked Miss Armbruster when the nurse came in to close the drapes for her nap.

"Tomorrow? Why, it's Saturday, that's what. One of our busy days here at the hospital. Crazy college kids try all their pranks on Saturday. The emergency room is a regular Grand Central Station on Saturdays."

Grumble, grumble, grumble, Jill thought, settling back against her pillows and wondering what had made Miss Armbruster so sour on life. But she didn't ponder the question for long; she was asleep in a matter of minutes.

When she awoke, she was aware of a slight feeling of depression. *I'm still stuck here in this prison of a hospital,* she thought. She knew she should be grateful that she was recovering so well, but still she longed for a familiar face or a telephone call from another human being.

And then there was a tapping on the window once again.

"Oh, bless you, you darling secret pal," Jill whispered out loud. Even though she hadn't yet

173

answered his last note, she guessed that there was another message from him. And she certainly was in need of a cheerful letter at this point!

She retrieved the note just before Miss Armbruster came charging back down the hall with Jill's dinner.

Dear Lady Down Below,

Please don't abandon me now. You haven't answered yet—or have you decided to be mysterious, now that I want to know all about you? What I care about is your mind—your intellect.

For instance what do you read? Shakespeare? Voltaire? Dostoevski? The Rosemont *Voice*? The supermarket tabloids?

And what are your preferences in music? And art? And how about the theater? I will tell you right now that I worship everything by Ibsen, and then at the same time I am entranced by the humor of Neil Simon. Guess I'm versatile.

P.S. I really *am* a homicidal maniac!

That was all. But it was enough, again, to make Jill laugh. As she picked at her meatloaf dinner she attempted to compose a mental list of her likes and dislikes. Shakespeare, of course; she could certainly

boast about her prowess with Shakespeare's plays—
and Joseph Conrad's *Lord Jim*.

But with art and music, she felt less certain. She
was beginning to suspect that her secret pal was
very bright with sophisticated tastes. And she
didn't know whether she could impress him with
her preference for Bruce Springsteen records.

Still, in the end Jill told the truth about herself,
as humorously as possible. She told her pal that she
couldn't pretend to be an intellectual snob because
she was an honest person, and a freshman at that.
She knew she had a great deal to learn in the next
four years at Rosemont. But for now she was simply
a girl with a fondness for *Macbeth*, exotic novels—
and an awesome collection of Springsteen records.

She managed to get the note into the cup, and it
was hoisted to the upper floor. But she heard no
more from her Dixie cup friend that night.

TWENTY

Saturday morning brought Jill a new wave of strength, enough so that she was almost her old self again. Beginning to feel bored out of her mind, she wished that Cassandra would deliver her books, so that she could at least start to catch up on her assignments.

There wasn't even the Dixie cup that morning. Jill felt dismal as she poked at her breakfast, watching the window and wondering if her answers had been too childish for the boy upstairs. Probably he had lost all interest in writing to her now that she'd admitted to being a freshman. Was she doomed to utter boredom for the rest of her hospital stay?

And that was when the cleaning lady came charging into her room.

"Oh, hi, Mollie," Jill said automatically, not really looking at the woman. "How are you today?"

"I'll bop you with a mop if you don't recognize me," said a voice that made Jill almost fall out of bed.

"*Toni!*" she said, gasping. "Toni, is that really you?"

"Sssh, keep it down," Toni scolded her. "You don't want that creepy nurse of yours to figure things out, do you?"

"Jeepers, Toni, it really *is* you!"

Jill stared at the apparition before her. Her petite friend was wearing the same sort of gray uniform that Mollie had worn the day before. She carried a mop and was pushing a housekeeping cart full of pails, cleaning solutions, and scrub brushes. And this little person had wrinkles and a head full of tightly twisted iron gray curls just like a bona fide senior citizen.

"I don't believe it. What's that on your head?" Jill whispered, trying not to laugh out loud.

"A wig, of course," Toni said with dignity. "Borrowed from the theater where I work. And look, I've even got makeup on! Makes me look pretty ancient, huh?"

"Oh, yes." Now Jill did start giggling. She couldn't help it. Her whole being was filled with such joy to see the face of a friend—and especially that of her very best friend—even if it was wrinkled and topped by a wig.

"I'd better make myself look busy," Toni said, starting to dust mop the room with great conviction. "You never know when that monster woman will show up, right?"

"Right. Oh, Toni, this is the happiest day of my whole life! How did you ever manage to do it?"

Toni was grinning triumphantly. "It's easy, when you're a born schemer like me. I got up early this morning—very, very early, I might add—and borrowed my mother's car. Drove here as speedily as I dared to, and I watched from behind a bush to see when the cleaning people arrived. Then I followed them to see where they kept their uniforms and carts and things!"

"You mean you just helped yourself to a uniform?" Jill asked, amazed. "Or did you knock somebody over the head, like in the movies?"

"Well, I thought of that, of course," Toni said seriously. "But it really wasn't necessary, because the cleaning people went out for a coffee break the first thing. And I asked Mollie if I could change with her. She was game, so the switch was on. I had spoken to Cassandra on the phone, and she told me how you were dying for company and how that sergeant was keeping visitors out. So I took a chance and marched right in."

Jill was shaking her head in disbelief. "You are a miracle worker, Toni Redmond. Who else but you would have thought of such a thing?"

"I had to see you," Toni said simply, giving the dust mop a vigorous shake and blowing dust right into Jill's face. Jill sneezed but never stopped grinning. "I mean, when I called your roommate she said you were so sick that somebody brought you here in a wheelbarrow. She also said the nurse won't let anyone near you, I said to myself, it sounds as though Jill really needs me."

"Oh, I did. I do. I'm so *glad* to see you, Toni, you have no idea—"

Suddenly the girls heard footsteps coming down the hallway.

"I hear a lot of commotion going on in here," bellowed the nurse, filling the doorway with her massive frame. "What's going on? Is that you, Mollie?" she asked quizzically.

Toni turned around to face Miss Armbruster. "No, I'm not Mollie," she said in a perfect imitation of a genteel, elderly southern lady. "I was sent from campus housekeeping to substitute for the regular girl today. And my goodness, I'd appreciate it if you would stay out of my way while I get these rooms spic and span."

Miss Armbruster gave a suspicious frown. "Substitute, huh?"

"Absolutely." Toni pushed the dust mop under the dresser and banged it so hard that one of the flower vases toppled over, spilling water across the room and splashing Miss Armbruster's spotless white shoes.

"You see?" Toni blustered, staring right at the nurse. "I do work so much better when no one is standing around trying to supervise. Can you come back later, Miss, er—"

"Miss Armbruster. Yes, I suppose I can. Is everything all right with you, Jill?"

"Oh, yes. Definitely."

"Very well, then." Miss Armbruster went away.

The two girls dissolved in giggles. "You did it, Toni!" Jill said in wonderment.

"Naturally. And now for the real surprise," Toni said grandly. She opened up the top of the housekeeping cart and pulled out a pizza box. "*Voilà*. How's this for a breakfast?"

Jill wanted to whoop with delight. "Much better than the oatmeal they gave me," she said, pushing away her breakfast tray. "But where do you get hot pizza at this hour of the morning?"

Toni waved away the question. "I have my sources," she said. "You know me. Nothing's too difficult for a friend."

"Toni, you're unbelievable." Jill took the piece of hot, fragrant pizza and ate it with a real appetite. Toni helped herself to a piece, too.

"So how are you now?" Toni asked, scrutinizing Jill carefully. "You don't look sick to me."

"I'm recovering." Jill couldn't talk because of the stringy mozzarella cheese filling her mouth. When she had finally swallowed, she said, "This is the most fun in the whole world. Maybe even as good as Paris or Venice, just because I needed you so badly!"

"Good." Toni opened another compartment of her cart. "And here's a Pepsi, and here's a stash of grape bubble gum for you. You'll have to hide it from you-know-who."

"Incredible," Jill said with delight. "But—no dessert?"

Toni gave her a do-you-think-I'd-really-forget glare and opened another drawer with a theatrical flourish. "Ta-dah—"

"Chocolate-chip cookies!" squealed Jill, then tried to tone down her voice. She certainly didn't want Miss Armbruster showing up now that the pizza box was out in plain sight!

They ate the pizza until they were completely stuffed. Then they began to catch up on the latest gossip while Toni fussed around, pretending to clean the room. Mostly Toni was interested in the flowers, and who had sent them.

"What? Nothing from that Ryan you're so crazy about?" she demanded.

"No," Jill said. "And Cassandra told him I was sick, too."

"Creep." Toni waved a feather duster across the windowsill, stabbing viciously at the radiator as if it were Ryan Davis. "Well, I'll find out the story about that guy, once and for all."

Jill held her breath. "What do you mean? Toni, what are you going to do?"

Toni's mysterious smile looked odd with the wig that had now slipped several inches down her forehead. "I mean that I came prepared, and I am going to visit this Ryan Davis today, that's what I mean."

"Oh, no. Say you won't do that. Please, Toni—"

"You can't stop me. I'll get his address somehow, if you won't give it to me, Jill. That part will be easy. And as for getting into his apartment, I came fully prepared."

"Fully prepared for what? Oh, Toni, no—"

"Natural vitamins, my dear Jill." Toni sounded pleased with herself. "I've got the whole act down. When I cease to be your cleaning woman, I become a salesperson for Happy Health Natural Vitamins. Door to door, of course. And I promise you I will solve this mystery for you, Jill."

Jill shook her head in awe. "You know, it is a good idea," she finally said. "I am dying to know what it is with that guy. I mean, I gave it my all and came up with zero. Maybe you *can* find out what his problem is."

"Of course I can" was Toni's breezy reply.

After the "cleaning woman" had departed, promising to come back, Jill's time stretched out endlessly. She was fidgety, squirming, worrying, and wondering what Toni could possibly be up to at Ryan's apartment.

Miss Armbruster was shocked to see that Jill hadn't eaten any of her oatmeal. "And the room doesn't look any too clean, either," she mentioned, looking around at the unwashed floors. "I'll have to tell Mollie that that substitute wasn't up to the job."

Jill was cheered by the sight of the dangling Dixie cup a little while later and almost bounded out of bed to get her latest letter.

"Hi, Secret Pal," wrote the mysterious patient upstairs.

I loved your honest note. You sound like a budding intellectual, and I think that you made the right choice coming to Rosemont College. Before you leave these hallowed halls you'll probably be a devotee of Mozart, but you may still be a fan of Bruce Springsteen. And why not?

I also love the humor you put into your notes, S.P. Have you ever thought of writing for the college newspaper?

At that, Jill suppressed a smile. Little did he know!

He went on.

I've been composing a limerick just for you:

> There once was a patient named Dan,
> Who sent notes in a small paper can,
> Up and down on a string,
> Some small hope he would bring,
> To a lass they call Dixie Cup Jan!

I guess that's pretty bad, but you can tell that I'm a sick man. Maybe if I didn't have this fever, I could write something more intelligent. Take care, dear pal. The day of redemption may soon be at hand.

P.S. I'm getting so delirious I even imagined that I smelled pizza! My days in this dungeon are taking their toll.

The guy is absolutely nuts, Jill thought with a flush of pleasure. She stared at his weird poem and wondered if she would ever know his name. But even if she didn't, he was doing her a world of good just the way things were.

She decided to surprise him with a sliver of leftover pizza stuffed into the Dixie cup. That would really make him think he was hallucinating!

She was starting to compose a poem for him when Toni came barreling back into her room.

TWENTY-ONE

Toni looked frazzled. "Well, I didn't sell any vitamins," she stated and plopped herself down on Jill's bed. She was wearing the gray wig still, but the wrinkles were gone.

"Toni, are you going to drive me crazy, or are you going to tell me what happened?" Jill was almost jumping out of her skin with curiosity.

"Of course I'm going to tell you what happened. What do you think I went to all this trouble for? Have I ever been the type to conceal information from you, Jill Gardner?"

"Toni, please." Jill was exasperated. *"What happened?"*

"Oh. Well, I assembled my saleswoman costume and drove over to that address. And I found his apartment, two-A—"

"Yes, Toni. And was Ryan there?"

"He certainly was. He answered the door, and just as I started my spiel about the vitamins, I could tell that he had someone there! Someone in the apartment with him!"

Jill's shoulders sagged. "Oh. Was it a girl?"

Toni looked thoroughly indignant. "It was! And I was sure angry, let me tell you. You know what I said to that creep?"

Jill's eyes fluttered closed. "No, what did you say?"

"I was in the middle of the vitamin commercial, like this, 'And you realize, sir, that the human body has a need for not only the trace minerals, but for a number of unusual elements such as copper and chromium—' And then I stopped, because I saw *her!*"

"Oh." Jill felt devastated. "Was she pretty?"

"Yes, I'd say so." Toni stared at Jill as though making a comparison. "Not as tall as you, but her hair might have been longer. Of course she didn't have your gorgeous color, with all those red and gold highlights, but still—"

"Toni. I don't think I want to hear about her. I do want to know what you said to Ryan."

"Well!" Now Toni really warmed up to her subject. "I dropped the vitamin sales act and I looked him right in the eye, and I said in my coldest, most evil voice, 'Do you realize that Jill Gardner is practically dying this very minute?'"

Jill let out a nervous giggle. "You didn't really." But, knowing Toni, she believed every word of it.

"So he gave me this real puzzled look as though I were some sort of escaped lunatic or something. Creep. I let him have it full blast. You know me, Jill, I have to speak my mind."

"Yes, I know you do."

"I put my hands on my hips and I said, 'Ryan Davis, you ought to know that Jill would be healthy right now, if she had taken my natural vitamins. Instead she's in the Rosemont infirmary.'" Toni was flashing fire from her eyes.

"Oh, thank goodness, you didn't demand to know who the girl was or anything."

"Well, I wanted to, Jill, but it seemed like a bit much. Anyway that's when my wig fell off."

"Oh, Lord. Did it really?"

Toni looked sheepish. "Yeah, well, they both thought I was a world-class weirdo by then. So I had to explain that I was your friend from Seattle and all that. They thought it was pretty funny, the way I sneaked into the hospital here—"

Jill moaned. "So now Ryan knows you just went there because—because I have a crush on him?"

"I'm afraid so, Jill."

"Oh, I'm going to die of embarrassment," Jill groaned.

"No, don't. He's really a neat guy, besides being so good-looking. He seemed to understand. Said he had had a crush on some older girl when he was a freshman here at Rosemont—which was part of the reason he flunked out."

"I don't want to hear any more," Jill said.

"Don't be silly. He said he liked you very much and hoped you would go on being friends. He'll call and talk to you as soon as you get released from here."

"Well, now I know the truth about Ryan. He already has a girlfriend. Oh, how humiliating."

"Stop it, Jill. You have a real neat friend there. Friends are important. And you know what else he said? He said that he always knew you were a terrific kid, but now he was sure of it—since you rated a friend like me!" At that, Toni grinned widely.

"Well, thanks for trying, Toni." Jill tried to smile, but ended up burrowing back into her pillows. "I guess what it boils down to is, I struck out again. First Craig, and now Ryan. I'm on such an unlucky streak these days—"

Toni jumped up off the bed, looking furious. "Will you stop that self-pity? You are not on an unlucky streak, I tell you. You have Ryan as a friend and what's more, there's a guy named Terry Somebody who's been hanging around outside this hospital every single day, just waiting for the latest bulletin on you. I bet you didn't know that, did you?"

"Well, I did, but—"

"But nothing. I met the guy. He's adorable, Jill. And he really has a thing for you, you know."

"I do know that, Toni, but—" Jill explained about the night at the pizza parlor and how she had realized, too late, that Terrence reminded her of Craig. "And, anyway, he's only a freshman, and you told me I should be out looking for older men, remember?"

Toni was silent for a moment. "I was wrong, then. A boy like Terry is worth ten of some old geezer. I had a nice long talk with him, and he seems like just your type, Jill."

"Sure. The Craig type."

"Jill, you're not being fair."

Jill nodded. "I agree, I haven't been fair with Terrence at all. I never gave him a chance, because I was so busy looking for the older man that Ryan represented. And then when I finally did give Terrence a try, it was only because subconsciously I saw him as Craig."

Toni began to fluff up her friend's pillows. "Well, I'm sure you can correct all that when you get out of here. Give the boy a chance and you'll be going to all the nice-people parties and things here on campus."

"Yes, Auntie Toni." Jill was finally smiling.

"You got that right! Boy, are you lucky you have me around to straighten out all your complicated love problems."

"What's going on in here?" Miss Armbruster had caught them red-handed this time. "What are you doing back here?" she demanded. "You don't even look like a cleaning woman. You look like a—a—"

"A college student?" Toni asked, her eyes rolling merrily.

Miss Armbruster sputtered. "You *are* a young person! Don't you know the rules? You aren't allowed to visit in an isolation room."

"Toni," Jill warned. "Don't get her more angry, please—"

But Toni was on a roll. "You know me, Jill. I try to be diplomatic, but really! I have to say what I think. And I think that you kept Jill much too isolated here. How can she ever get better?"

"Young lady, I hardly think that you—"

"I know," Toni said. "I don't have a medical degree or anything. But I know a few things about people recuperating. After all, we nursed my dad back to health after his heart attack. And I know that a girl like Jill needs to see people in order to get better. Can't you see that?"

"Well—perhaps," the nurse admitted. "But what gives you the right to dress up in a costume and come in here?"

"I have no right, I suppose," Toni said. "But it really was the only way. And just look at the nice pink roses in your patient's cheeks."

The nurse looked at Jill. "Yes, I guess so, but—"

"I'll be going now, anyway," Toni said, smiling and collecting her shoulder bag. "My business here is concluded."

"Yes?" said the nurse, still stunned.

"There's just one thing," Toni added. "I'd say you need someone to clean out this patient's wastebasket. Gosh, just take a look. There's an empty pizza box, of all things, in there!"

And with that, Toni blew Jill a kiss and bustled out.

TWENTY-TWO

"I can't imagine how you've made such a quick recovery," Dr. Walker said as he listened to Jill's chest on Monday. "You must have had some very good care here, Jill."

"Oh, yes, you could say that," Jill said, smiling. She firmly believed that seeing Toni had been like a giant shot of penicillin, because she'd been feeling totally healthy ever since the incident with Toni and the pizza and the chocolate-chip cookies.

"I'll let you go back to the dorm this afternoon, if you'd like," the doctor told her, and Jill almost took a flying leap out of the bed.

"Would I ever!" she said joyfully. "I can't wait to see good old McGregor Hall again."

"But you will take better care of yourself from now on, won't you?" the doctor asked. "No more running around with a heavy chest cold or ignoring a fever?"

"I promise," Jill said.

"Jill was a fairly good patient, Doctor," said Miss Armbruster reluctantly. "I suppose it wasn't her fault that that crazy girl from Seattle came here—in disguise."

Dr. Walker tried to hide a grin from the nurse. "Sounds like a fascinating story," he said. "But I guess as long as Jill was a model patient, that's all that counts."

"Well," went on Miss Armbruster. "She *did* disobey us once, by going to the window, but I put a stop to that immediately!"

Jill tried to keep a straight face. Little did the nurse know how often she had gone to that window. In fact, the Dixie cup was dancing around on its string outside right this minute! She'd just have time for one farewell note to her secret pal, who had come to be someone really important to her.

When the doctor and nurse had gone, she scribbled her note.

Dear Secret Pal,

They're sending me home now, so I guess this is goodbye forever. I feel as though I know you very well, and yet, of course, I don't know you at all. So all I can say is—thank you. You kept me going when things were really rough.

She didn't sign it.

And though the Dixie cup disappeared, no answer came to her note while she was still there. *So that's that*, Jill thought, feeling curiously let down. *It's all over*.

An hour later she was packed and ready to go. She was surprised when Cassandra and Terrence arrived for her.

"Oh, I didn't need an escort to go home," Jill said, blushing. "I hope you didn't plan on using that wheelbarrow again."

"No." Terrence looked utterly serious. "We managed to get a dump truck for you, this trip."

"Hmmmph," muttered Miss Armbruster, listening to the whole exchange. "You college kids. Never take anything seriously. Not even pneumonia!"

When the three of them had gotten clear of the room, they dissolved into laughter.

Her friends escorted her back to McGregor, where most of the kids in the dorm were assembled on the front porch or hanging out of windows. "Welcome home!" shouted Marcie. "About time you got back here to work, you bum!" Robert yelled.

"This is so nice," Jill said to Cassandra and Terrence. "I mean, this feeling that people know me, and sort of like me—"

"Of course they like you!" Cassandra sputtered as they entered their room. "I don't know why you worry about it so much, but since you do, you've got your wish. People do like you, Jill Gardner." Then, in an imitation of Miss Armbruster's grumbling voice, she said, "Honestly! College kids!"

Terrence stayed in their room, looking as comfortable as though he lived there. Jill was just beginning to wish he'd go away, so she could plop down on her bed for a short nap, when Heather came in to tell her she had a telephone call.

"Someone named Ryan Davis," Heather said. "Isn't that the guy we fixed you all up for that night?"

Jill shot a worried glance at Terrence. But he looked at ease. He said, "No problem. I've always known about Ryan. Big deal. So you had a crush on somebody older." His green eyes sparkled at her. "I told you, I don't give up that easily, Jill."

Oh, boy. College life is so crazy and complex, Jill thought as she went to the hall telephone. Things like that never seemed to happen at her home.

"Hi," said Ryan's voice. "I just wanted to wish you a welcome home."

"Oh—thank you."

"And I'm sorry I never sent a card. Or flowers. I really did mean to, but—"

"I know. My friend Toni told me."

Ryan laughed, his deep rich laugh that had been so appealing to Jill all this time. "She's quite a character, that friend of yours. Came here dressed like an old lady, with a weird wig, pushing vitamins, and then suddenly she was yelling at me like a crazy person—"

"I know. Toni is one of a kind."

"She's good people," Ryan said sincerely. "And so are you, Jill. And that's why I called, too. I want to say that I really mean it about being friends. That's not just a brush-off phrase."

"Why—that's very nice," Jill said. "But—"

"But nothing. I'd like to take you to a psychology lecture that's coming up next week. She's a really good speaker, a noted textbook author who will probably be of interest to you. What do you say?"

"But Toni says you have a girlfriend. That girl who was with you at your apartment."

"Trish?" Ryan began to laugh. "Is that why your friend Toni was glaring at me? She thought—? Oh, that's a good one!"

"Why is that a good one?" Jill asked.

"Because Trish is one of my younger sisters. They take turns coming to visit me. They like to help me clean my apartment."

Just as I wanted to, Jill thought.

"Well, what do you say about the psych lecture? Is it a date?"

"Um—I think I'd like that. Yes, Ryan," Jill answered.

"There's just one thing. Please, please don't let those dorm friends of yours dress you, this time. Okay? I'd much rather be with Jill Gardner, the eighteen-year-old, than that overpainted suburban matron who went with me to the spaghetti dinner."

Jill laughed out loud. "It's a promise, Ryan." And she noticed that she could say his name without feeling her heart go all crazy. *Hey*, she thought. *Maybe I'm growing up.*

Terrence was ready to leave when she returned to her room.

"You need your rest, Miss Gardner," he said cheerfully. "It's always exhausting when you first come out of a hospital."

He turned at the doorway and looked directly at Jill. "You haven't heard the last of me though. I hope you know that."

"Good." Jill gave him a sincere smile.

Jill couldn't forget her Dixie cup friendship. She daydreamed, on and off, about the boy in that upstairs hospital room and still wondered if she'd ever learn his name.

So she was thoroughly intrigued when she saw the following poem in the personals column of the Rosemont *Voice* that week:

Dixie Cup Jan, oh where can you be?
I'd like to believe that you're thinking of me.
These Shakespearean couplets are easy to write,
I compose them all day and into the night.
But friendships on paper are doomed to be bland,
A meeting in person I think would be grand.
If you're curious to know my name at all,

Then dial this phone number, and give me a call.

Your Secret Pal

It was followed by a campus phone number.

Jill stared at the silly poem for a long, long time. She was torn by conflicting emotions. On the one hand, she really *did* want to know who her secret pal was. But on the other hand, Jill knew it would be hard for her to call up a strange boy. And even if she did, she'd probably sound silly and childish to him. Her secret pal had sounded like a great reader and a total intellectual. How could she help being a disappointment to him?

Finally she showed the newspaper to Cassandra and explained her dilemma.

"Hey, I can't tell you what to do," Cassie said. "But it sure is an exciting situation." Cassie's eyes were bright with interest. "I know what you should do."

"You think I should call," Jill guessed.

"You're not the shy little butterfly that you think you are, Jill. Why, I've read your terrific columns, and I've seen you charge off and join the water polo club. Even chasing after Ryan, when you were positive he was the man you wanted. I told you once before, I admire you for all that, you know."

"You really do?" Jill was amazed.

"Sure. You're dynamite, Jill." Cassie grinned. "Now if only we could harness some of your

197

dynamite for one of our causes, like saving the whales, we could make the world a better place."

Jill felt very buoyed up by Cassie's praise because Cassie wasn't the sort to hand it out easily.

"How about you, Cassie? You've been changing somewhat, too, lately. Playing water polo?"

"Yes, and I even managed to get a crush, on Paul, the team captain. He's asked me out, as a matter of fact, and I'm going."

"Oh, Cassie, I'm happy for you. It means you're extending yourself to people. And when you talked about becoming a doctor or a vet—"

"Forget that," Cassandra said sharply. "Let's get back to your problem. Are you brave enough to call up Dixie Cup Dan?"

"Okay, maybe I am. Maybe I *should* call this guy."

"Of course you should," Cassie said. "You've got nothing to lose!"

Later that evening Jill picked up the phone and dialed the number she had seen in the personals column.

The phone rang several times before anyone picked it up. "Hello," a deep voice finally said.

Jill gulped. *Here goes nothing*, she thought. She cleared her throat. "Um—is Dixie Cup Dan there, please?"

There was silence on the other end, then, "Don't tell me—could this be Dixie Cup Jan?"

"You got it," Jill replied, wondering why his voice sounded familiar.

"Well, Jan, I'm glad you called. You know, you really saved my sanity in the hospital. I've got to meet you. We could have a cup of coffee. Look, Dixie Cup Dan's only an alias—my real name's Jake Randall—"

Jill nearly dropped the phone. *Jake Randall! The* Jake Randall. Boy wonder writer. She couldn't believe it.

Somehow she managed to tell him her name and got through the rest of the conversation without sounding too dumb, she thought.

Dear Toni,

You'll never believe this, because I still don't.

Remember that secret pal I told you about, the one upstairs who sent me all the crazy notes in the hospital? My secret pal is none other then Jake Randall, *the* famous Jake Randall.

Now maybe this is not world shattering to you, but you can imagine how it feels to me, Toni, being a fledgling writer on the Rosemont *Voice*. And, Toni, he was so nice on the phone! He remembered who I was right away, and he said we definitely had to meet to have coffee together someday soon.

Now don't start thinking of this as a romance for me. It won't be, at all, because Jake is some kind of a big playboy, according to the other seniors. I remember that from my interview for the "Last Year's Girl" column. So if I have coffee with him it will be strictly as a friend, and we can talk about writing and other literary things. I can't imagine anything I'd rather do, Toni!

I've learned something in these past few weeks. A girl and a guy can be friends—just friends. And that's a pretty wonderful thing I'm starting to think. I mean, as you yourself said, I have Ryan Davis and Terrence for friends, and I count myself really lucky. They're just as interesting as Jake, in their own ways.

So I think I've made a lot of progress, thanks to you and Cassie and all these new men in my life. I'll always be grateful to you, Toni, for showing up at the hospital that day and cheering me up.

Of course the drill sergeant may never recover from the incident, but we can't help that. Probably did her some good.

Enough about me and Rosemont College. I won't even ask that you write to me, because Thanksgiving vacation is coming up soon and I just found out that I'll be home for a whole week. Can you believe it? A whole week, back home in Seattle! I can't wait.

All my love, Jill

Special Offer
Buy a Bantam Book
for only 50¢.

Now you can order the exciting books you've been wanting to read straight from Bantam's latest listing of hundreds of titles. *And* this special offer gives you the opportunity to purchase a Bantam book for only 50¢. Here's how:

By ordering any five books at the regular price per order, you can also choose any other single book listed (up to $4.95 value) for only 50¢. Some restrictions do apply, so for further details send for Bantam's listing of titles today.

Just send us your name and address and we'll send you Bantam Book's SHOP AT HOME CATALOG!